WALT DISNEY
PRODUCTIONS'

HERBIE THE MATCHMAKER

A novel by
JOE CLARO

Based on the Walt Disney Productions'
television series teleplays written
by ARTHUR ALSBERG and DON NELSON
and based on characters created by
GORDON BUFORD

SCHOLASTIC BOOK SERVICES
New York Toronto London Auckland Sydney Tokyo

This book is for Tasha, Nicole, Noel,
Danielle, and Chris

ISBN 0-590-32691-0

12 11 10 9 8 7 6 5 4 3 2 1   11   2 3 4 5 6/8

Printed in the U. S. A.   01

WALT DISNEY
PRODUCTIONS'

HERBIE

THE

MATCHMAKER

Chapter 1 _____

"No, sir," Jim Douglas said into the phone. "My racing days are over."

The swivel chair squeaked as he leaned back and put his feet up on the desk. He listened to the bank manager talking on the other end.

"That's right, Mr. Harrington," Jim said. "It's a promise. No more racing. I've moved on to bigger and better things."

As his eyes surveyed his office, Jim thought he might like to take back that "bigger." The office was bigger than a telephone booth, but not by much. And the desk took up most of that space; its top was buried under a mound

1

of forms, textbooks, local telephone books, and general clutter.

Jim was tilting the seat back against the wall on which he had hung the operating license for his business, the Famous Driving School.

Jim shut his eyes to all this. He had to concentrate on his sales pitch.

"The business is thriving, Mr. Harrington," he said brightly. "We think now is the best time to expand."

The license in the center of the wall was surrounded by photos taken in different parts of the world. They showed various people photographed with Jim Douglas— and Herbie.

The biggest picture showed Jim proudly holding the Grand Prize from the annual Monte Carlo auto race, his free hand resting on Herbie's roof. Herbie was Jim's VW bug—and his oldest friend.

There were those who thought Jim took Herbie a little too seriously. They said he treated his car as though it were human. Jim would just smile when he heard these remarks. They should only know how human Herbie was.

"No, Mr. Harrington," Jim was saying, "I'm not talking about a *big* loan." He crossed his fingers and took a deep breath. "Just enough for a down payment on a few late-model cars. To go with the other late-model cars we have."

While Jim was telling this fib to the banker, one of his "late-model" cars was pulling up in front of the office. Actually, it was the only "late-model" car the driving school owned. It was Herbie, the other retired racer (besides Jim) in the family.

On his roof, Herbie wore a removable, magnetized light that announced the Famous Driving School. The VW pulled up to the office door and came to a gentle stop.

Bo Phillips, Jim's assistant instructor, sat in the passenger seat. Behind the wheel was a little woman, old enough to be a great-grandmother. Bo got out, hurried around to the driver's side, and opened the door.

"That was some driving, Mrs. Gurney," he said, helping her out. "It's hard to believe it was your first time."

"I never would have waited so long," she said, "if I'd known it was going to be this easy."

Just then Jim appeared in the doorway. "Well," he said, "two smiling faces! I guess you did okay, Mrs. Gurney."

"Try *great*!" she said enthusiastically.

"Her son bought her the lessons for her birthday," Bo said.

"Eighty-five years old today," Mrs. Gurney said.

Herbie, who never liked to be left out of a conversation, threw in a comment. His horn honked out the six notes of "Happy Birthday."

Mrs. Gurney looked at the car, then at Jim. Jim spoke up before she had a chance to say anything.

"Just part of the service, Mrs. Gurney," he said nervously.

Before Jim had to explain further, a car drove up to the curb. The man at the wheel waved.

"Here's my son," Mrs. Gurney said. "I can't wait to tell him about the lesson." She paused and looked at Herbie. "But I don't think I'll tell him about the horn."

"See you next week," Jim called, as she walked slowly to the curb. Then he turned to Bo and asked, "How was she?"

"Got a perfect score," Bo said. "She never shifted a gear. She never found the brake. And she didn't open her eyes through a single intersection."

"Nice going, Herbie," Jim said, patting the car on the hood. "You love playing up to the old ladies, don't you?"

"Sure," Bo said, "while they're making an old man out of me!"

"Bo," Jim said, "that wouldn't happen if you had a little more faith in Herbie."

Bo looked unconvinced. They'd been over this ground many times before.

"You see," Jim explained, "every once in a while, a car comes off the production line that's a little different from the rest."

"I hear you," Bo said, as Jim got into the car. "But every once in a while, when I'm squeezing between a cement mixer and an oil truck, I'd settle for a run-of-the-mill car with dual controls."

Jim pulled Herbie into a parking space next to the office and got out of the car.

"How did you make out with the loan?" Bo asked. "Will they come up with the ten grand?"

Jim looked sadly at Bo.

"Five grand?" Bo asked. Still no answer. "Twenty-five hundred?"

Jim shook his head.

"Zero, huh?" Then Bo's face brightened. "Doctor Bo is in the know," he said, pulling a piece of paper from his pocket. "I have your cure right here."

"What's that?" Jim asked, looking at the paper.

"Your entry blank for the Long Beach Grand Prix this weekend."

"Doctor Bo," Jim said slowly, "the answer is *no*!"

"Are you kidding?" Bo said, his voice rising. "Look at this prize money!"

Suddenly, Herbie backfired. The noise startled Bo, and he dropped the entry form. Herbie backed up over the form, squirted oil on it, and returned to where he had been.

Jim bent down and picked up the oil-soaked form. He held it up for Bo to see.

"There's Herbie's comment," Jim said. "Too many races won, and girlfriends lost. We're looking to settle down, Bo. I'm afraid Herbie and I are through with racing."

Jim turned and headed toward the office. Bo followed him angrily.

"Well, *I'm* not through with *eating*!" he said. "And eating takes money. What are the chances of getting paid for this week?"

Jim stopped and turned to him, but said nothing.

"For last week?" Bo asked timidly. "The week before?"

"Tell you what I'll do, Bo," Jim said. "I'll go by the bank this afternoon—"

"I have a better idea," Bo said. "Don't go *by* the bank. Go *in* it!"

                    *   *   *

Two hours later, Jim drove up to the bank and looked for a parking space. He saw a car ready to pull out of a space, and he stopped behind it to wait.

So Jim was just sitting idly, drumming his fingers on the steering wheel, when a man in a Halloween mask came out of the bank.

A Halloween mask! Jim stared in disbelief.

The masked man carried a large, over-loaded sack in one hand and a gun in the other. Then a second man, also masked, came out of the bank. This one had a gun pressed into the back of a woman, who was hurrying before him. She looked terrified.

The first thief flung himself into the front seat of a waiting car. His accomplice pushed the woman into the back and climbed in, and then the car raced down the crowded street.

"Where are the police when you need them?" Jim yelled.

For an answer, Herbie revved his engine and took off after the robbers. He had to do some fancy weaving to avoid hitting cars and pedestrians.

"Herbie!" Jim yelled. "Are you crazy? Think about your fenders! Think about *my* life and limbs!"

Herbie thought only about the car he was

after. He zoomed diagonally across a parking lot to the street the thieves had turned into.

His timing was perfect. He came out of the lot and into the street just as the robbers' car was approaching. The driver swerved to avoid ramming into Herbie and rammed into a tree instead.

The thieves jumped out of the car as Herbie drove up. One of them aimed his gun right at Jim. Herbie flipped open his front hood, knocking the gun out of the robber's hand.

The sound of sirens filled the air, and the thieves turned and ran. Herbie fired the spare tire from his trunk. It rolled down the street, straight for the thieves, and bowled them to the ground.

Two patrol cars screeched up from opposite directions. Four policemen jumped out and stood over the robbers. One of them bent down and took possession of the sack of money.

Jim got out of Herbie and hurried over to the car that had smacked into a tree. He opened the rear door and offered his hand to the woman hostage.

"It's all over," Jim said, helping her out. "You're fine."

"I wish someone would tell my knees

that," she said, trying to smile.

Jim put his arm around the woman's waist to keep her from losing her balance, and found it an enjoyable task. She was very attractive.

A policeman came up to them. "You okay, Miss?" he asked.

"Yes," she said, her voice shaking.

He turned to Jim. "I heard you did some fancy driving to stop them."

"Yeah," Jim said. "Normally, it would have earned me six tickets and thirty days in jail."

The policeman smiled and went back to the scene of the arrest. The woman took a deep breath and seemed to get control of herself.

"I owe you a big thank you," she said.

"I didn't have much choice," said Jim, looking at Herbie. "You might say I was 'driven' to do what I did."

"Well, you saved my life," she said.

Jim looked into her eyes and smiled. "I can't think of anyone I would rather have saved."

"I wish I could do something in return," the woman said.

"Well," Jim said, reaching into his pocket, "since you mention it." He handed her his business card. "You might know someone who needs driving lessons."

"Jim Douglas," she said, reading the card. "There's a Jim Douglas who teaches driver education at the high school."

"We are one and the same," Jim said.

"You have a Julie MacLane in one of your classes."

"That's right."

"I'm her mother. Susan MacLane."

"Pleased to meet you, Mom," Jim said, grinning.

"You know," Susan said, looking at his card, "maybe I *can* give you some business. Julie could use some private driving lessons."

"What about your husband?" Jim asked. "He isn't a coward, is he?"

Susan paused. Then she said, "More like a deserter. We've been divorced for over five years."

Well, Jim thought. She's not only pretty, she's also unattached.

"I assure you," he said, "Herbie would be delighted to teach Julie."

"Herbie?" Susan asked. "I was sort of hoping *you* would do it."

"Uh . . . Herbie's our car. And I'd be happy to teach her."

"Great!" Susan said. "I . . . uh . . . don't

suppose you could start this afternoon?"

"I just had a cancellation," Jim lied.

"Good," Susan said, smiling. She took out a pencil and wrote on a small pad. "Here's my address."

Jim took the slip of paper. Susan smiled and walked off.

"See you at four!" he called after her. Then he stood there, grinning foolishly, until she was out of sight.

Herbie wanted to tell Jim he knew what was going on. His front hood flapped up and down, and his whole frame pulsated with excitement.

"You're absolutely right, Herbie," Jim said. "She is one *very* attractive lady!"

Chapter 2 _____

Jim and Herbie moved slowly along a quiet, tree-lined street, on their way to Susan MacLane's house. Jim was humming "Put on a Happy Face." Herbie purred and puttered along with him.

"Another first, Herbie," Jim said. "This is the first time you've ever seen me dress up for a student's *mother*."

He glanced into the rearview mirror and straightened his tie. Then he saw a red light up ahead, moved his foot from the accelerator to the brake, and gently pressed. Herbie came to a stop at the corner.

"Flowers, Mister?"

Jim turned his head and saw a boy on Herbie's passenger side. He held several bunches of flowers in his hand. His head was just about even with the top of Herbie's window.

"No, thanks, son," Jim said.

"Special today," the boy said. "Only five dollars a bunch." His hand reached into the car, holding a small bunch of flowers.

"No," Jim said, "I don't think I—"

He stopped because he saw Herbie's window slowly raising itself. It went just far enough to hold the boy's arm inside the car without hurting him.

"Herbie!" Jim said under his breath. Then he looked at the arm extended into his car and at the boy's pleading face.

He reached into his pocket, then took the flowers, and replaced them with a five-dollar bill. The window slowly went down, and the boy withdrew his arm.

"I have another special today," the boy said. "Boxes of candy."

"No, thanks," Jim said. "The flowers are enough."

He shifted into first gear and stepped on the gas. Herbie didn't move. Jim tried second gear. Herbie stayed dead still.

Jim reached into his pocket and took out another five-dollar bill. He sighed and offered it to the boy.

"What good are flowers without candy?" he said weakly.

"He'll be here any minute, Julie," Susan called from the kitchen.

Her fifteen-year-old daughter was in the living room, lying on the couch. At the window, Julie's brother Matthew, twelve, was craning his neck to see down the street.

Suddenly, there was a loud noise as Robbie, their seven-year-old brother, came bounding through the front door. "He's here!" Robbie announced.

Julie got up from the couch and dragged herself over to the window. Extra driving lessons were not her idea of a good time.

"Oh, no!" she groaned, her eyes widening at what she saw outside. "He's driving that *little car!*"

"That's the car he teaches in after school," Susan said, as she came into the living room.

"Mother!" Susan wailed. "I can't learn in that kind of car! It's embarrassing!"

"Yeah," Matthew said in support. "I want to learn in a TR-7."

"I think it's a neat car," Robbie said, looking out the window. "There was one just like it in the circus. Twelve clowns got out of it."

"Exactly!" Julie said, as Jim pulled up to

14

the curb. "A clown is what I'll feel like when I drive in it!"

"Julie," Susan said soothingly, "I owe my life to that man."

"Then *you* take the lessons!" Julie said.

"I'll take them!" Robbie offered.

The doorbell rang, and Susan went to answer it. When she opened the door, Jim was standing there with both hands behind his back.

"Hello, Jim," Susan smiled.

"Oh—" Jim began. He looked into the faces of three youngsters where he had expected to see only one. "This is? . . ."

"*This*," Susan said, laughing and gesturing toward her family, "is all of us. You know Julie. Matthew and Robbie, this is Mr. Douglas."

"Hi!" Matthew and Robbie said together.

"Hello," Jim said.

"Was your car ever in the circus?" Robbie asked.

"No," Jim said with a chuckle. "But he was in a few races before we retired."

"Could it beat a TR-7?" Matthew asked.

"Maybe not," Jim said. "But he *can* take a whole family for a driving lesson."

"Hey!" Robbie squealed. "I'm gonna get a driving lesson!"

"And *I'm* gonna get a headache," Julie mumbled.

"Go on, kids," Susan said. "It'll be fun."

The boys ran out to the car. Julie threw one last, long-suffering look at her mother. Then she turned dramatically, and followed her brothers outside.

Jim smiled at Susan. "I was hoping the mother would come, too," he said.

"She'd love to," Susan said. "But she's kind of busy right now."

"How about a private lesson later?" Jim asked. "One that would involve dinner?"

Susan hesitated. Then she said, "That's very nice of you. Really. But maybe another time."

Jim looked disappointed, but not beaten. He brought both hands from behind his back.

"You might as well take these now," he said, holding out the flowers and the candy. "They might not keep until another time."

Her mouth dropped open, and he handed her the gifts. She was too surprised to say anything. Jim gave her a little salute and went out to join the kids.

Julie was driving on a four-lane street, not far from her house. Jim sat in the front next to her, the two boys in the back.

"Your left turns are fine," Jim said.

"Does that mean the lesson's almost over?" Julie asked.

Jim laughed and said, "Your enthusiasm could use a booster, though."

Julie looked into the rearview mirror. "Oh, no!" she moaned. "It's Jason and Raymond from school!"

Jim and the boys turned and looked. A customized chariot was right behind them. The driver and the passenger were both students in one of Jim's classes.

Jim turned back in time to see the stop sign at the corner they were approaching. He was about to point it out to Julie, when she suddenly ducked down out of sight.

"Hey!" Robbie yelled. "You're gonna get us killed!"

Matthew looked into the side street to see if any cars might be heading for the same intersection. Both boys expected the car to shoot through the stop sign. Instead, Herbie came to a smooth stop at the corner.

"Man!" Matthew said, letting out the breath he was holding. "We *never* would have stopped without dual controls."

Robbie hopped out of the seat and looked at the floorboard under Jim's feet. Then he looked at Jim.

"Where *are* the dual controls?" Robbie asked.

Jim looked down at Julie, who was still hiding from sight. Then he said to Robbie, "Fortunately, a car like Herbie practically drives itself."

By now, the chariot had pulled up beside them.

"Hey, Julie!" It was Jason, the driver.

Julie slowly sat up and looked straight ahead.

Raymond, the passenger, leaned out of his window and said, "Mr. Douglas? Is this a new way to teach her to keep her eyes on the road?"

Jason added, "She was probably doing it through a hole in the floor. How about burning a little rubber, Mr. Douglas?"

Without waiting for an answer, Jason tore past the stop sign, tires screeching. Jim looked after the car angrily.

"We'll have a review lesson on road etiquette tomorrow!" he said.

Jim took a few seconds to calm down. Then he said to Julie, "Make a right here."

She turned into the side street. Just as she came out of her turn, a gold Mercedes convertible cut in front of Herbie.

Herbie had to do a fancy step to avoid hitting the sports car. The VW wound up half on the sidewalk.

"Speaking of etiquette!" Jim yelled. "Who is *that* turkey?"

As the boys looked out the rear window, the Mercedes stopped and began to back up.

"It's Uncle Randy!" Robbie said. "Mom's boyfriend."

"And *Mom*," Julie said, watching the car from the rearview mirror.

The sports car backed up to within a few feet of Herbie. The man who got out on the driver's side was a little older than Jim. His suit looked expensive—just as his car did.

Susan stayed in the flashy gold car, looking a little embarrassed. The man walked over to Herbie, and everyone got out.

"Hi," the man said brightly, extending his hand to Jim. "Randy Bigelow. Sorry about what happened. Just trying to catch up with you."

"Hi, Uncle Randy," Robbie said.

Jim reluctantly shook hands with the man. "I'm Jim Douglas," he said. "We were out for a lesson."

"Yes, I know," said Bigelow. He sounded as though he were speaking to an audience, not to a person. Jim was going to learn that Randy Bigelow always sounded that way.

"I owe you my thanks," Bigelow said.

"For what?" Jim asked.

"For saving my little lady here."

"Your . . . uh—"

"And my mother also thanks you," Bigelow went on, "for saving her bank a considerable amount of money."

"Ohhh," Jim said, realizing now who he was talking to. "Well, I keep a little loose change there myself."

"Glad to hear it," Bigelow said. "Mother will be, too. She's chairman of the board, you know. In fact, Susan was there to have lunch with us. Of course, those hoods interrupted our plans."

"Yes," Jim said. "Luckily, I interrupted theirs."

"That you did," Bigelow said. He seemed eager to get the conversation over with.

"Well," he said, rubbing his hands together, "if the lesson is over, I thought I'd take the children for some treats."

Jim was about to say the lesson had just begun. But before he could, Robbie and Matthew had hopped into the back of the sports car, ready to take off for their treats.

Jim turned to Julie, whose hangdog expression made it impossible to prolong her agony anymore.

"Lesson's over," he said, and she gave him a little smile.

"Oh, by the way, Douglas," Bigelow said. "That was a quaint idea, the flowers and the candy. Does that go with all the lessons, or just with the *special* ones?"

The last few words were slippery with sarcasm, and Randy's smirk added to the effect. He got into his car and started it. As he pulled away, his car kicked dirt and gravel onto Herbie's hood.

"Thanks a lot, Herbie!" Jim said, looking after the flashy car. "Five dollars for flowers, five dollars for candy! Next time, don't pick a woman who has three kids and a boyfriend with a sports car!"

Herbie wasn't really listening. His whole body was vibrating. It might have been just a way to get the dirt and gravel off his hood. Or he might have been shaking with anger at the man who had put the dirt and gravel there.

Chapter 3 _____

Early that same evening, Herbie pulled up to the curb in front of a small apartment house. Wearily, Jim got out. He was tired after the long day, and disappointed about Susan.

Jim walked into the lobby of his apartment house. He pressed the elevator button, and the doors slid open. As soon as he had stepped into the elevator and was out of sight, Herbie's engine started up.

Herbie pulled away from the curb and headed down the street. A man walking by glanced at the driverless car. He looked away, then did a double take.

Herbie had gone around the corner. The

man decided he hadn't seen what he thought he'd seen, and he hurried home.

The gold sports car pulled up in front of Susan's house. Bigelow hopped out and bounded toward the house, all glee and cheerfulness. He rang the bell, and when the door opened, he stepped inside.

Herbie quietly turned the corner onto Susan's street. He pulled up behind the sports car and gave it a little nudge. Then another nudge, and another.

The sports car began to roll. Herbie pushed it down the street in the direction of a house near the end of the block.

The house had a beautiful, lush, green lawn. To keep it that way, the owner watered it for hours each day. At this moment, a small army of sprinklers was lavishly watering the lawn.

Herbie gently nudged the little convertible toward this house. Then he guided it into the driveway, which was getting as much water as the beautiful grass.

Back at Susan's house, Bigelow paced in the living room, nervously checking his watch every few seconds. Susan came down the stairs.

"I'm ready," she said, smiling.

Bigelow glanced out the window. His eyes widened and his mouth fell open.

"My car!" he gasped. "It's gone!"

Bigelow ran outside and looked down the block. The first thing he saw made him want to burst into tears. His beautiful, little gold sports car was being drenched by somebody's lawn sprinklers!

The second thing he saw caused a fierce anger to boil up inside him. It was the rear of *that car*, turning the corner past the house with the sprinklers.

Bigelow stood there sputtering for several seconds. Susan had followed him out of the house, and she came up to him now.

"Is anything wrong?" she asked. "I'm sorry I kept you waiting—"

"Sorry!" he bellowed. "I'm sure your friend Douglas isn't sorry! Look what he's done with that ridiculous Volkswagen of his! He's pushed my beautiful car into that . . . that . . . rain forest!"

Bigelow was in tears as he ran toward his car. Susan followed him. Matthew and Robbie ran out of the house and shot down the street after them.

"Did you say Jim Douglas did that?" Susan asked, trying to keep up with him.

"I saw him sneaking away in his car!" Bigelow screamed, waving his arms.

As they reached the driveway, Susan said, "I don't believe it! Why would he do a thing like that?"

Bigelow stopped and turned to her. His face was bright red, his eyes teary. "Why?" he said, gritting his teeth. "Jealousy, that's why! It can turn a grown man into a destructive child!"

Matthew and Robbie finally caught up with them. They stared in disbelief at the car.

"Uncle Randy?" Robbie said. "How come you parked here?"

Matthew got as close as he could without getting soaked himself. "The upholstery is ruined," he said. "And the carpeting. And the leather."

"The whole evening is ruined!" Bigelow cried, pressing his hands into the sides of his head.

Jim took a TV dinner from the freezer and turned the oven on. The phone rang, and he walked over to answer it.

"Hello."

"Hi. Susan MacLane."

"Oh! Hello!" Jim said with much more enthusiasm.

"I knew you'd be home," she said.

"Did you, now?" Jim said. "Well, I didn't know you'd be calling. But as long as you did, I'm glad I'm home."

"Then you didn't just drive by my house?" Susan asked.

"Only in my mind," Jim said. "About a dozen times."

"I can't imagine why," Susan said. "I mean, after this afternoon."

Jim laughed. "You mean the three kids and the sports car?"

"The sports car has been canceled for the evening," Susan said. "Something happened to it. My date is off."

"Oh," Jim said, smiling. "Does that mean you'll give old flowers-and-candy a chance?"

"I'd love to," Susan said.

"Don't move!" he said. "I'll be right there!"

While he was putting on a clean shirt, Herbie pulled into a space across from Jim's building. He sat there and waited.

Jim came running out of the apartment building, holding his tie. He started to cross the street to where Herbie was. Then he stopped and looked at the spot where he thought he had parked Herbie. Another car was parked there. Jim gave the car a curious look. Then he shook his head and walked over to Herbie.

"Our luck must be changing, buddy," he said, knotting his tie. "We have a date. Would you believe it, something happened to the other guy's car."

He patted Herbie on the rear hood and stopped talking. He looked suspiciously at the car.

"Your engine's warm," he said. "Where have you been, anyway?" Then, brightening, he said, "Never mind. I don't think I want to know."

He hopped in and drove to Susan's house.

Jim hadn't suggested a restaurant. They were just driving and enjoying each other's company. He didn't even notice that Herbie was pulling up to the entrance of a very fancy—and very expensive—French restaurant.

"My goodness!" Susan said, as they stopped. "You don't care *where* you take a woman for dinner!"

Jim realized where he was. He glowered at Herbie's dashboard and said, "Oh, I care, all right!"

The parking valet walked up to the car on

the driver's side. Jim looked up and was astounded to see that the man in the little red jacket was Bo.

"Bo! What are you doing here?"

"Shhh!" Bo said. "I'm working nights. They have an interesting custom here. They pay me! You know—with money?"

He bent down a little more, so he could see into the car. He and Susan exchanged smiles. Then the smile faded and he looked at Jim.

"Speaking of money," Bo said, "what are *you* doing here? You can't even afford to have me park your car!"

Jim had no idea how he was going to get out of this spot. Then Susan solved the problem for him.

"I hate to disappoint you, Jim," she said. "But I don't think I'm dressed properly for this restaurant."

Jim quietly let out a sigh of relief. "Well," he said, "I wouldn't want you to be embarrassed, Susan."

Herbie's motor started up. Jim held on to the steering wheel, but he wasn't really in control of the car.

"Where else can we go?" Susan asked.

"Why don't we just wait and see?" Jim said uncertainly.

* * *

A half hour later, Herbie came to a stop on a cliff overlooking the lights of the city. Both Jim and Susan were munching on hamburgers as Herbie's motor turned off.

"One of your favorite spots?" Susan asked playfully.

"Well . . . uh . . ." Jim said, "not since high school." He reached toward the ignition. "We don't have to stay," he said.

"Wait till I finish my burger," Susan said.

"Oh. Sure." He leaned his head back and tried to relax. Then he tried to think of a good topic for conversation.

"Uh . . . Julie has the makings of a good driver," was the best he could come up with.

"Probably gets it from her father," Susan said. "He's a race car driver. Maybe you've heard of him. George MacLane?"

"George MacLane?" Jim said, thinking. "I think I've gone up against him. Years ago, when I was racing."

"Believe it or not," she said, "he's still racing, somewhere in Europe. But if you don't mind, I'd rather not talk about it."

"Subject closed," Jim said. "Let's talk about—"

"The car's moving!" Susan interrupted.

Herbie backed out, slowly spun around,

and parked in a different direction. Through the windshield, they now had a terrific view of the full moon.

"Let's talk about the moon!" Jim said, grinning.

Susan smiled. "I think we'd better talk about getting me home."

"Right you are," Jim said.

Herbie sat in front of Susan's house, waiting for Jim. The only other car parked along the street was a Cadillac, a few houses down. The driver sat slumped in the front seat, trying not to be noticed.

The driver was Randy Bigelow. He was hiding in his "other" car, trying to find out what was happening inside Susan's house.

The front door opened, and Jim and Susan stepped out. The street was quiet enough for Bigelow to hear their conversation.

"You handled the third degree very well," Susan said.

"Well," Jim said a little nervously, "facing three kids isn't as bad as being grilled by the Internal Revenue people."

"You've been very sweet," she said. She leaned forward and kissed him on the cheek.

"Careful," Jim said, grinning. "I could learn to like that."

They stared at each other for a moment. Then Jim turned and hurried toward his car. As he was about to get in, Herbie's horn blasted out the first four notes of "Here Comes the Bride."

Jim turned to Susan with an embarrassed smile. "Just kidding!" he said.

"Just kidding?" Bigelow mumbled in his car. He watched Susan blow a kiss to the VW as it rolled down the street.

"We'll see who's kidding, Douglas!" he said out loud. "You teach driving, do you? Well, I have a lesson I'm about to teach *you!*"

Chapter 4 _____

Randy Bigelow parked his Cadillac two blocks away from Jim's apartment house. He got out, locked the car, and walked to Jim's place.

The sun hadn't been up for very long, and there were very few people on the street at this time of morning. Bigelow ambled over and stood beside Herbie. He tried to appear casual as he checked to see that no one else was walking about.

For the son of a banker, Bigelow had some pretty shady friends. His mother had never allowed him much freedom. As a result, he began to lead a secret life way back in high school.

He was attracted to people who led the kind of life he wasn't allowed to lead. He could be found tagging after street-corner tough guys, private detectives, pilots, and—yes—even race car drivers.

These people weren't often attracted to him. But Bigelow always had money, and that can make up for a lot of shortcomings.

So, even though he was the son of a banker, Bigelow possessed some pretty startling skills. His shady friends had taught him a lot over the years.

One of the things he'd learned was how to jimmy open the locked door of a car. That explains how he came to be sitting inside Herbie at this very moment. He was bent double under the steering wheel, using another skill he'd picked up—he was hotwiring Herbie, to get him to start without an ignition key.

Bigelow had learned his skills well; Herbie's engine kicked over. Bigelow sat up and grabbed the steering wheel with both hands.

"And now, Mr. Douglas," he said angrily, "a lesson in what happens when you tangle with Randy Bigelow!"

He put Herbie into gear and drove down the street. When the car was up to forty miles per hour, Bigelow's eyes began to shine, and his face became distorted by an evil smirk.

He spotted a large oak tree up ahead. Pressing down on the accelerator, he aimed Herbie at the tree. He closed his eyes and got ready for the crash.

Five feet before reaching the tree, Herbie swerved to the right and continued down the street. Bigelow opened his eyes and stared ahead in astonishment.

"I . . . missed . . . the . . . tree?" he said out loud. "How could I miss a *tree*?"

His eyes shone with even more determination, and his smirk got uglier. One block ahead was the entrance to a large restaurant. Six large metal garbage cans lined the curb outside, as they did every morning at this time.

Breathing heavily, Bigelow aimed Herbie straight for the cans. Then he stepped on the accelerator.

Two seconds before contact, Herbie swerved to the right. This time, the driver's door swung open just as the car swerved.

Bigelow went sailing out of the car and into the middle of the line of garbage cans. Herbie made a U-turn and his door slammed shut. The cans toppled over and covered Bigelow with their contents.

Herbie pulled up to the space he'd left a few minutes earlier. Jim came out of his building, climbed into the car, and drove off.

A few blocks down the street, Jim passed a neighborhood restaurant. He passed it every morning, so he didn't even bother to look. That's why he didn't see the mess near the curb. And he certainly didn't see Randy Bigelow, half a grapefruit on his head, waving a fist at the little VW bug.

"How could you even *think* of going on a date?" Julie said to her mother at breakfast. "You're practically engaged to Randy!"

"That doesn't mean I can't like someone else," Susan said, buttering a slice of toast. "And I *do* like Jim Douglas—a little."

"I like his *car!*" Robbie said through a mouth full of cereal. "A *lot!*"

"Mom," Julie said, "he's struggling to keep his business afloat. He isn't exactly what you'd call wealthy. I'm going to be worrying about college tuition in a little over a year—"

"And I need braces," Matthew chimed in.

"Maybe we could marry Randy," Robbie said thoughtfully, "and keep Jim's car."

As they collected the dishes from the table, Julie made one last effort.

"Mom," she said, "the bottom line is that

he's a race car driver. And you know what that means."

"He gave that up long ago," Susan said, putting the dishes into the dishwasher.

"Did he really?" Julie said sarcastically. "Didn't you make that mistake once before?"

Susan's eyebrows went up, and she turned to face her daughter. "A lecture?" she said. "From my fifteen-year-old daughter?"

"Just something for you to think about, Mom," Julie said. Then she turned and left the room.

In front of the driving school, Jim was hosing Herbie's front wheels. He was also wondering about Bo, who was late for work once again.

"You're a real mess, Herbie," Jim said. "Looks like you lost your way in a salad bar."

He turned the hose off and reached inside the car for a scraper. As he did, Bo came hurrying up to him.

"Sorry I'm a few minutes late," Bo said.

"A *few*?" Jim said, looking at his watch. "I have 8:45."

"You kidding?" Bo said. He rolled up his sleeve to reveal four watches. "I have an 8:20, an 8:23, an 8:29, and an 8:15."

Jim blinked at the sight of Bo's arm. "What is this?" he asked.

"More part-time work," Bo explained. "I sell these door-to-door for Alexander Jewelers. How was the date last night?"

Herbie answered him by tooting "Here Comes the Bride."

"Come on, Herbie," Jim said, laughing. Then he turned to Bo and said, "She sure is a terrific woman, but it was just a date."

Jim bent down to clean Herbie's wheels. Bo grabbed a cloth and began wiping off the hood and roof.

"We didn't do much of anything," Jim went on. "But I had a great time."

"Uh-oh," Bo said. "That sounds like the most serious kind of date."

Again Herbie tooted "Here Comes the Bride."

"That *would* be serious, Herbie," Jim said. "There are three kids to support. The middle one needs braces, and the daughter will be in college soon."

"Sounds like a money problem to me," Bo said, wiping off the rear hood.

"Then there's the boyfriend," said Jim. "Old moneybags. I just can't compete with what he has to offer."

Bo stopped working. He pulled a new entry blank from his pocket.

"You would be able to," Bo said, "if you had Herbie's winnings from the Long Beach Grand Prix."

Jim looked up at him. "No," he said seriously. "Not even if I did have the entry fee."

A few minutes later, Jim sat at his desk, staring at the phone. Bo was outside putting air into Herbie's tires.

Jim reached for the phone, then quickly pulled his hand back. He stared at it for a few more seconds, reached again, hesitated, then picked up the receiver and dialed.

After two rings, he heard Susan's voice. "Hello?"

"Hi, Susan. This is Jim. I hope you don't mind my calling."

"Mind?" she said brightly. "I was just trying to decide whether or not to call you."

"I had a great time last night," he said. "But I woke up with . . . well, with a few questions."

"Yeah," she said. "I guess I have some myself."

"First question: How about meeting me for coffee this afternoon?"

"I hope they're all that easy," Susan laughed. "The answer to that one is yes. I'll be downtown shopping. Can you pick me up at Grover's Drugstore about four?"

"You got it," Jim said happily.

Susan hung up the phone, grabbed a jacket, and left the house. As she got into her car and drove off, Julie peeked out through the curtains of her bedroom window.

When she was sure her mother was gone, Julie went downstairs, picked up the phone, and dialed. She waited, nervously drumming her fingers on the table, as the phone rang on the other end.

"Hi," she said suddenly. "It's Julie. I did what you said. I warned her about him being a race car driver and all. She said he's through with racing."

"Do you believe that, Julie?" Randy Bigelow asked on the other end of the phone.

"I don't know what to believe," Julie said, a look of pain on her face.

"Then you owe it to your mother to find out," Bigelow said.

"I . . ." Julie stammered, "I . . . just want to do the right thing."

"You *are* doing the right thing," Bigelow said, smiling evily. "You just do what I've told you. I'll take care of the rest."

Chapter 5 _____

The roar from the crowd was deafening. The three lead cars raced around the turn, followed closely by Herbie.

On the inside lane, Herbie moved into third place. Within moments he passed the next car and took over second place.

The roar became louder as Herbie pulled up even with the lead car. They were one hundred yards from the finish line.

Another increase in the level of the roar. Fifty yards to go. Herbie fell behind by a foot or two. Twenty-five yards left, and Herbie turned on his final burst of power.

The fans went wild as Herbie crossed the

finish line inches ahead of his competitor.

The roar stopped suddenly. The room went dark, and someone switched off the movie projector. Jim flipped on the lights, and the driver education students clapped, showing their delight with the film they'd just watched.

It was a large room, specially designed for driver ed classes. A pair of sliding doors led out to the school parking lot. A wide space near the blackboard allowed the teacher to have a car in the room for demonstration purposes. Right now, that space was occupied by Herbie.

There were twenty students in the class. Julie MacLane was one of them. Also in the class were Jason and Raymond, the two boys who'd challenged Jim to a race in the street.

"That's all the entertainment for today," Jim said to the class. "I just wanted to show some of you hotshots how that 'funny little car' can take care of himself."

"You mean *in his day*," Julie said, hoping to get Jim riled up.

"In *any* day!" Jim shot back. Julie had clearly hit her target.

"You mean you're still racing?" Julie said, still trying to bait him.

"No," Jim said firmly. "Herbie and I are retired."

"Kinda like an ex-heavyweight champ, huh, Mr. Douglas?" Raymond called from the back. Jim was just about to agree, when Jason added, "Fat, slow, and over the hill."

That one got to Herbie. He began to vibrate a little. So little, that only Jim noticed. He walked over and gently put his hand on the hood to calm Herbie.

"Not exactly," Jim said to Jason. "Herbie still has what it takes. He just doesn't have to prove it anymore."

"Yeah," Raymond said, laughing. "He sure didn't prove it to us yesterday."

"I've already talked to you about that, Raymond," Jim said. "It wasn't the time or the place for a challenge."

"How about the drag strip, then?" Julie asked. "The guys are going out there this afternoon."

"Yeah," Jason said. "Come on out, Mr. Douglas. Show us a thing or two!"

The bell rang, and Jim spoke over it. "Sorry, fellas. I have more important things to do this afternoon."

"Yeah," Raymond called out, as everyone

filed into the hall. "He has to drive old Herbie out to retirement village."

In response to the laughter from the students, Herbie began to tremble angrily. Jim patted him on the roof.

"Easy, Herbie," he said softly. "Take it easy, old fella."

It was the wrong thing to say. The trembling increased.

"Sorry!" Jim said. "Just a figure of speech, pal. A slip of the tongue."

Outside the school, Julie left her friends and headed toward a Cadillac parked across the street. She bent down on the passenger side to talk with Bigelow.

"I think it's working," she said. "But I'm not sure."

Bigelow looked down the street and saw Herbie—with Jim driving—going through the intersection. He smiled a little.

"Let's find out, shall we?" he said in his oiliest voice. "Hop in."

They followed at a distance, but it wasn't hard to keep the VW in sight. When Herbie pulled up in front of the drugstore, Bigelow stopped almost a block behind. Then he saw Susan coming out of the store.

"Well," he said, trying to seem pleased, "it looks as though our timing is perfect."

Jim went around and opened the passenger door for Susan. When she got in, he closed the door and smiled at her.

"I'm glad you could make it," he said.

Then they both said, at the same time, "I have a few questions."

"Like about a boyfriend," Jim said, laughing.

"And about racing," Susan said, with a smile.

"Let's go somewhere and talk about it over coffee," he offered.

"Good idea," she said.

As Jim walked around to the driver's side, Jason's customized chariot pulled up alongside Herbie.

"Looks like Mr. Douglas has been to the car wash," Raymond said loudly.

"How can you tell?" Jason asked, just as loudly.

"Because Herbie's all washed up!" Raymond yelled. And the chariot roared away.

Herbie was vibrating again as Jim got in. Jim looked a little concerned. He knew what Herbie was like when he was angry.

"Just some kids from school," Jim said to Susan. Then, talking more to the dashboard than to her, he added, "Don't pay any attention to them!"

Jim knew immediately that his advice was going to be ignored. Herbie took off and turned the corner after Jason's hot rod.

Susan looked straight ahead, her forehead creased in curiosity.

"Are you following those boys?" she asked, uncertainly.

"Who, me?" Jim said. "No, no. I mean, yes, in a way. You see . . . uh . . . there are lots of good coffee places down this way."

Then he spoke to the dashboard again. "And we are *definitely* going to stop for coffee!"

"Yes," Susan said, smiling, "I heard you the first time."

"I just wanted to be sure *everybody* did," Jim said to the dashboard.

Jason's hot rod was headed out of town. Herbie was close behind it. At a respectable distance, Bigelow and Julie kept Herbie in sight.

"There's a Black Kettle up ahead," Susan said. "It's quiet and comfortable, and they have really good coffee."

"Great!" Jim said to the dashboard. "The Black Kettle it is. *We'll stop there.*"

As they approached the restaurant, Jim tightened his grip on the steering wheel. He got ready to turn into the parking lot.

Herbie had other ideas. He zoomed right past the restaurant.

"Or maybe," Jim said, admitting defeat, "we'll look for a better place."

Susan looked at him, a little puzzled. Then she looked ahead, where Jason was turning off to a dirt road.

"You *are* following them, aren't you?" she said.

"Well, yes," Jim said, trying to keep himself from looking like a prize fool. "I . . . I guess I am. You see—"

"Is this a race track?" she asked. The puzzlement had now turned to annoyance.

"No, no, not at all," Jim said quickly. "It's more like a . . . a drag strip."

"I don't get it," she said, with even more annoyance. "What are we doing here?"

Several cars were lined up at the starting line, ready for a drag race. It was less than a mile from start to finish. The race was a contest of acceleration and instant speed.

"You see," Jim said, trying to talk his way out, "they're my students. I was a little worried about them. They can get pretty wild sometimes. I thought they'd need some supervision."

Herbie drove up to the starting line. Jim gripped the wheel. Susan sat stiffly beside him, staring icily into space. She couldn't believe what was about to happen.

Jim spoke desperately to the dashboard again. "One thing we're definitely *not* doing here is racing. *We are not going to race!*"

The signal went off, and Herbie made it clear that Jim just didn't know what he was talking about. They took off with the rest of the cars, Jason's included.

"Oh, wow!" Julie said, hopping out of Bigelow's car. "My mother in a drag race?!"

"Yes, Julie dear," Bigelow said. "That puts the lid on Mr. Douglas. Now watch me drive the nails into the coffin."

The race was over in seconds. Herbie, of course, had come in first, just ahead of Jason. A dozen kids rushed up to surround Herbie as Jim and Susan got out.

"Hey, Mr. Douglas!" Jason called. "Your car really *does* have it!"

"Yeah!" Raymond said, slapping Jim on the back. "Talk about showing us a thing or two!"

"I have to see that engine!" Jason said. "I still can't believe it!"

He opened the rear hood to admire Herbie's inner workings. The other kids gathered around to do the same.

"Well," Susan said, trying to keep her anger below the boiling point, "you really showed *me* something."

"Uh, listen," Jim said weakly, "I'm sorry about all this."

Beginning to lose control, Susan said, "What was all that talk about being through with racing?"

"Let me explain—"

"Forget it! You just did! The same way my husband did for twelve years! And *he's* still addicted to racing, too!"

"Susan—"

"Don't 'Susan' me! You racing nuts are all alike! No sense of responsibility! Undependable! Playing your childish little ego games—"

"Hey, slow down—" Jim said.

"All you can think about is racing, racing, *racing*! Why do you think I left him? He wasn't a father *or* a husband!"

"Now just a minute," Jim said, his own anger beginning to swell. "*I'm* not your husband either!"

"That's the *good* news!" she shot back.

"Well, let me tell you—"

"Some show, Douglas," Bigelow said, grinning as he walked up to them.

Startled, Jim looked at him curiously. "What are you doing here, Bigelow?"

"You and that car!" Bigelow said, laughing. "What a performance! I bet you'd even stand a chance in that Long Beach Grand Prix."

"Well, yeah," Jim said, still not sure what was going on. "I probably would at that."

"But of course," Bigelow continued, "according to Susan, you've quit racing."

Jim gave Susan an angry look and then turned back to Bigelow. "I might be in that race," he said, "if I had the entry fee!"

"Well," Bigelow said smoothly, "this may be your lucky day."

He reached into his pocket and took out a checkbook. Then he tore out a check that had already been written.

"A little reward check from Mother's bank," he said, handing the check to Jim.

Jim reached out, then hesitated. Julie looked on with great interest.

"Perhaps this reward will cover the entry fee," Bigelow said. "That is, *if* you're serious about being able to compete."

Jim looked at Susan, who stared angrily past him. Then he reached out and grabbed the check from Bigelow's hand.

"I'm as good as in it!" he said to Bigelow. Then, to Susan, "Does that answer your question?"

"Yes," she said coldly. "And *this* should answer yours."

She stepped over to Bigelow and took his arm. Then she began leading him away from the drag strip.

Bigelow called over his shoulder, "Keep that funny little horn tuned up, Douglas. Some day soon it will be playing "Here Comes the Bride" for Susan and *me!*"

Still angry, Jim watched them walk off. His first reaction was relief that the ugly scene was finally over. Then he realized that something very nice was also over.

"Herbie," he said, "I have a feeling that we've just outsmarted ourselves."

Jim turned to see Herbie squirting water on his windshield and brushing it away with his wipers. Jim patted Herbie's hood.

"I know what you mean," he said. "Tears do seem like the right reaction, don't they?"

Chapter 6 _____

Herbie's tears turned out to be more appropriate than Jim would have wished. Two weeks later, on a Saturday morning, Randy Bigelow was loading some of Susan's luggage into the back of his sports car. He and Susan were going to be married in just a few hours.

Matthew and Robbie sat on the curb, watching Bigelow load the car. Neither of them looked too excited about the day ahead.

Matthew asked, "Do we have to be at the wedding, Uncle Randy?"

"Of course," Bigelow said cheerfully. "Your mother wants you there."

"Do we have to go on the honeymoon, too?" Robbie asked.

"Over my dead body," Bigelow said, arranging one of the suitcases.

"I'd rather stay here and watch Jim Douglas and Herbie race today," Robbie said.

"Me, too," Matthew added.

Bigelow froze at the mention of those two names. His eyes narrowed.

"You mention their names once more," Bigelow said through clenched teeth, "and—"

Instead of saying what was on his mind, Bigelow took his anger out on the luggage strap, pulling it tight enough to cause a crease in a suitcase.

Upstairs in her bedroom, Susan was packing some last-minute items in a small overnight bag. She moved slowly, pausing now and then to stare into space. Julie stepped out of her mother's closet holding a blouse.

"You forgot to pack your favorite blouse," she said.

"Oh," Susan said, snapping back to what she was doing. "I don't know that it's really my favorite."

Julie looked at her thoughtfully. Then she asked, "Is it because you wore it that night with Jim Douglas?"

"Of course not," Susan said quickly, busying herself with her packing. "I haven't given Jim Douglas another thought."

She turned away from Julie and bent over her bag. Julie looked worriedly at her mother.

At the same moment, Jim sat at his desk at the driving school. While Jim filled out the entry form for the Grand Prix, Bo paced nervously back and forth in front of the desk.

"Jim," Bo said, "I know this is just another race to you. You and Herbie have won them all. I've seen the films." He pointed to the wall behind Jim. "And I've looked at these pictures thousands of times. But for me—it's a first. It's a brand-new experience—"

"I know," Jim said, forcing a smile. "You might get paid."

Bo thought about that for a second. Then he said, "You know something? It's not the money. This whole thing just makes me feel tingly all over. I think of standing there at the finish line with you and Herbie, the reporters, the fans and everybody . . ."

"Not everybody," Jim said sadly, looking out past Bo.

Julie sat on the bed and watched her

mother. After a long silence, Julie said, "I guess he'll be racing today."

"Listen," her mother said, turning from her packing, "I'm getting married today! That's the only thing on my mind. Neither racing nor Jim Douglas interests me in the slightest."

But Julie couldn't let it drop. "Suppose he really meant to quit racing, Mother," she said. "Suppose he was—sort of *pushed* into this race."

"He's doing what he wants to do," Susan said, practically throwing her stockings into the overnight bag.

"I hope we *all* are," Julie said to herself.

"You know," Jim said to Bo, "it won't be a sure thing out there. I don't know if Herbie really has his heart in it."

"Herbie?" Bo said. "Or you? Let's face it, Jim. You're still thinking about that woman with the three kids and the sports car."

"*Me?*" Jim said, a little too loudly. "Wrong, Bo. She made her choice. And I made mine."

"Believe me, Julie," Susan said, "I've thought it over very carefully. It's the best thing for all of us."

"I just want you to be sure, Mom."

They heard Bigelow's horn honking. Susan gave her daughter a little smile.

"I'm sure, Julie. Go tell Randy I'll be right down."

Julie gave her mother a long look, then turned and left the room.

Susan looked at herself in a wall mirror. "I'm sure," she said to her reflection. "Really I am."

Bo sat at the desk looking worriedly at Jim. Jim was now doing the pacing. Back and forth he walked across the tiny office, back and forth, back and forth.

"Listen to me," Bo said glumly. "If you're thinking of pulling out of this race because of that woman, tell me now. Don't break my heart later."

"I'm not pulling out of any race!" Jim insisted, still pacing.

"You're sure?"

"I'm *sure!*"

Bo watched Jim pace for a few seconds. Then he said, "I'll get the gear."

When Bo was outside, Jim stopped pacing and stared at a wall. "Of course I'm sure," he said weakly.

Then he walked to the phone, picked it up, and dialed Susan's number. At precisely the same moment, Susan picked up her phone at home to call him.

Jim heard the busy signal and hung up before Bo came back inside. Susan heard the busy signal on her end and hung up, too. Then she went outside to join her family and the waiting groom.

He was standing on the passenger side, holding the door open for her. In his best public-speaking voice he said, "We're expected at noon, and I'd prefer to be on time, Susan. Mother has gone to a lot of trouble to make the arrangements."

Susan got into the car. Bigelow closed the door and walked around to the driver's side. He never noticed what was behind a tall clump of bushes halfway down the street.

Herbie was hiding behind those bushes, his antenna bent in the direction of Bigelow's sports car. The antenna picked up everything Bigelow was saying.

"The Chapel of the Chimes is a special place," he said as he got into his car. "They don't have weddings there every day, you know."

"I'm sorry," Susan replied. "I just keep thinking I've forgotten something."

Bigelow started his car. "Whatever it is,"

he said, "I'll buy you a new one in Santa Barbara after the wedding."

Herbie had all the information he needed. His antenna straightened and withdrew. He listened as the sports car pulled away with a roar, and then he sped down the street in the opposite direction.

Jim was climbing into his driving suit. Bo, wearing his pit-crew coveralls, hung up the phone and smiled.

"The pit crew is all set," he said, rubbing his hands together. "Stacey, Carruthers, and Ferguson. A little on the old side, but all good men."

"Now all we need is luck," Jim said, pulling up the front zipper of his suit.

"Luck?" Bo grinned, pointing to himself. "You're looking at it!"

Neither of them saw Herbie quietly slide back into the space where they'd left him. They both heard his horn, though. It blasted out "Here Comes the Bride" three times.

"Boy!" Bo said. "Herbie is sure fired up!"

Jim was listening to what the horn was playing. "Yeah," he said. "But about the wrong thing."

They picked up their gear and carried it

outside. Herbie's engine was running. And his horn kept tooting "Here Comes the Bride" over and over.

"Forget it, Herbie!" Jim yelled over the horn. "Forget it once and for all! I am *not* marrying that woman—now or ever!"

The horn stopped, startling Jim. Then he looked pleased that Herbie had actually done as he'd been told.

"Good," Jim said, climbing into the car. "Now, come on. We have a race to win."

"It'll be a snap!" Bo said excitedly. He bent to remove a hubcap. "Let's get you stripped down for action, Herbie!"

Bo got one hubcap off, but that was all. Herbie rudely pulled away and shot down the avenue.

"Hey!!" Bo shouted, waving his arms. "I'm going, too! And anyway—Long Beach is the other way!"

But Herbie was already out of sight. Bo flung the hubcap to the ground. It clanged twice and then rolled to the curb.

"I knew it!" he screamed at the top of his voice. "I *knew* one of them would break my heart! But I didn't think they *both* would!"

On the highway to Santa Barbara, Bigelow slowly tooled along in the right lane. He was smiling slightly and humming to himself.

Matthew watched the other cars zipping by them. He'd been keeping his mouth shut since they left the house. But he couldn't stand it any longer.

"Why don't you floor it, Uncle Randy?" he said.

"We have plenty of time," Bigelow said, smiling out at the road ahead of him.

Robbie grumbled, "We'll probably be driving forever."

"Yeah," Matthew said, slumping down in his seat.

"We'll have no unhappy boys," Bigelow announced loudly. "What is this, a wedding or a funeral?"

Then he looked at his passengers for a reaction. The boys looked angry, and Julie was looking uncertainly at her mother. Susan stared straight ahead, with no expression on her face. Bigelow's smile faded, and he drove on in silence.

Jim tugged at the wheel, punched at the dashboard, and kicked at the brake pedal. None of it did any good.

Neither did yelling. "Herbie!" he'd bellow. "Where are you taking me?"

He did this every ten seconds or so, as a

change of pace from tugging, punching, and kicking. Herbie just zoomed along.

They pulled onto a highway, just as Jim was finishing one of his screaming fits. He was about to start tugging, punching, and kicking again, when he noticed the highway sign.

"*Santa Barbara?*" he cried in disbelief. "We're going to Santa Barbara?!"

" 'Here Comes the Bride,' " Herbie honked.

"Herbie, I'm *not* getting married!"

" 'Here Comes the Bride,' " Herbie honked again.

There was silence for a few seconds, as they tore along the highway. "Oh!" Jim finally said. "*She's* getting married! I guess she's marrying—"

"WHONNNK!" Herbie honked. It was the kind of sound you get when you put your tongue between your lips and blow.

"That's who I figured," Jim said. "They deserve each other."

Jim thought that over for a second. He decided he didn't really mean it. But it was still none of his business.

"What do you think you're going to do, Herbie?" he said. "Stop it? We don't even know what time the wedding is."

But Herbie *did* know. And he had his own

way of telling Jim. The hands of Herbie's dashboard clock began to spin crazily. They stopped at twelve.

"Okay, so it's at noon," Jim said, feeling that he'd once again been put in his place. "But who are you kidding? We'll *never* make Santa Barbara by noon!"

That was the wrong thing to say. Herbie was already firing along, but he threw in an extra burst at Jim's remark.

Jim's head was thrown back by the force of the jolt. "Ohhhh, Herbie!" he moaned. "You're gonna get us killed!"

Chapter 7 _____

"How much longer?" Robbie groaned, as the sports car moved along at the same slow, steady pace.

"We're nearly there," Bigelow said, trying to sound cheerful for the benefit of his gloomy riders.

"I can't wait," Robbie said.

"Yes," Bigelow said, beaming. "We're all looking forward to the wedding."

Robbie twisted in his seat. "I mean I *really* can't wait," he whined. "I have to go to the bathroom!"

Bigelow turned and gave him a nasty look. "We'll stop at the next gas station," he said.

*   *   *

Herbie was on a ramp leading to the local road that would take them into Santa Barbara. The way things looked, he would be on that ramp long after the wedding was over.

"Forget it, Herbie!" Jim said. "This weekend traffic will tie us up for hours! I *told* you there was no way—"

But Herbie had already found a way. The ramp was separated from the service road by a metal fence. Herbie had spotted a gate in the fence. And the gate was open.

He pulled onto the grass and rode past the cars stuck on the ramp. He reached the opening, eased through it, and tore out along the service road.

Again Jim was thrown back into his seat. Again he moaned. And again Herbie ignored him and burned his way to Santa Barbara.

With no highway to follow, Herbie really had to use his imagination. After bouncing along a bumpy back road for miles, Jim found himself riding through a pitch-black tunnel.

"I didn't know where we were going before!" Jim screamed. "Now you *really* have me in the dark!"

But not for long. They sailed out of the tunnel into the bright sunlight and came out in the middle of a park—on a bridle path, in fact. At the moment, the bridle path was being used by several horseback riders.

Herbie slammed on his brakes, kicking up dirt and cinders as he screeched to a stop. The noise and the sight of the car weren't very good for the horses. Three or four of them reared up and whinnied.

Herbie backed off while the riders calmed the horses down. Then the horses continued on down the path.

"Wrong kind of bridle path, Herbie," Jim said.

"Honk?"

"Never mind. Just a pun. Too sophisticated for a youngster like yourself."

The "youngster" then took off through the park. They were still miles from the Chapel of the Chimes, but Herbie was not about to give up now.

Mrs. Bigelow stood outside the chapel, nervously tapping her foot. She was a woman who was not used to being kept waiting, even by her own son.

Nervously, she fingered the edge of the fur stole she was wearing around her neck. Her diamond ring and gold bracelets glistened in the bright sun.

She tensed when she saw the Mercedes coming up the street. Her son pulled up in front of the chapel, and everyone got out.

"Sorry we're late," Bigelow said, as he walked up to his mother. Then he threw a nasty look in Robbie's direction. "We had to make an unscheduled stop."

"Well," she said haughtily, "I've done the best I could on such short notice."

"Knowing you, Mother," he said, kissing her cheek, "I'm sure everything will be perfect."

"Thank you, dear," Mrs. Bigelow said, accepting his kiss. "A perfect wedding for a perfect son." Then, smiling slightly at Susan, she added, "And his lovely bride."

Susan forced herself to smile back, while Julie glumly watched the whole unpleasant scene from the sidelines. Matthew and Robbie ran up the chapel steps to see what all the fuss had been about.

Herbie screeched to a halt in front of a sign that read, ROAD CLOSED. CONSTRUCTION AHEAD. The sign wasn't quite truthful, because there was no road in front of them. It had been torn out so the workers could dig deep holes for installing sewer pipes.

"This is it, Herbie," Jim said, exhausted. "*Now* will you turn back?"

Herbie answered Jim by backing away from the sign and heading straight for a line of huge sewer pipes. They ran along the side of the demolished road. End to end, they formed a road of their own, at least for an adventurer like Herbie.

The little car picked up speed as it bounced into the first hollow pipe. For this stretch of the ride, Jim's moans echoed back at him off the walls of the giant pipes.

"Do you, Randy, take Susan to be your lawful wedded wife?" The minister looked up at Randy and smiled.

Meanwhile, Herbie slowed down as he approached an old, rickety wooden bridge. Then he seemed to decide that slowing down was a bad idea. He zoomed forward and raced across the bridge with lightning speed. Jim's eyes were tightly shut.

"Do you, Susan, take Randy to be your lawful wedded husband?"

Fired up for the final lap, Herbie ripped into the street where Mrs. Bigelow had stood waiting, only minutes before.

"If anyone knows why this man and this woman should not be joined in holy wedlock . . ."

Herbie reached the chapel entrance. He made a sharp right turn and aimed himself at the open double doors.

". . . let him speak now or forever hold his peace," the minister said.

At that moment, Herbie came charging into the chapel, down the wide center aisle, tooting his horn.

"Beep, beep, beep!"

"Herbie!" Robbie squealed.

The little car pulled up to the altar and stopped just behind the wedding couple. Jim's door flew open, and he fell out of the car. Except for Robbie, who yelled Herbie's name again, everyone was too astonished to speak.

After a number of sputters, Bigelow finally found his tongue.

"What in heaven's name do you think you're doing, Douglas?" he said between clenched teeth.

Jim was brushing himself off, more embarrassed than he'd been in a long time. He straightened up and tried to look as dignified as he could under the circumstances.

"Interrupting something, I guess," he said pleasantly.

"My wedding!" Susan said angrily.

"Oh, sure," Jim said, still trying to sound as though he did this sort of thing every day. "You're marrying—"

"WHONNNNK!"

Jim pointed to Bigelow to indicate who Herbie was talking about.

"You're darn right I am!" Susan said firmly.

"Go right ahead," Jim said. "Don't let me stop you."

"Uh . . . Mr. Bigelow," the minister said softly, "perhaps we could continue. I have another wedding at one-thirty."

"Continue!?" Bigelow roared. "With this man . . . and his ridiculous car . . . standing at the altar like . . . like a couple of bridesmaids?!"

"I kind of saw myself as the best man," Jim said calmly. Then he looked deep into Susan's eyes and added, "In more ways than one."

Bigelow missed the look that Susan and Jim were exchanging at that moment. But

Julie saw it, and she began to smile.

"I don't see you," Bigelow yelled, "as anything but *out*!"

He stormed over to Herbie and began pushing him back up the aisle. Jim and Susan continued to stare at each other.

"Perhaps I can help," the minister said pleasantly to Bigelow.

He stepped down to Herbie's side. Bigelow stood at the hood, and they both began to push.

A heavy squirt of oil oozed from somewhere underneath Herbie. It covered Bigelow's shoes and made him lose his balance.

Bigelow slipped and fell. He wound up lying under Herbie, his legs between the front wheels. Susan began to laugh, but quickly covered her mouth.

Robbie and Matthew laughed out loud as Bigelow struggled his way out. He stood up, slipped twice more, and then leaned on Herbie to keep his balance.

"Douglas," he said, seething, "aren't you overdue for that race at Long Beach?"

"Well," Jim said, smiling, "I seem to have found something more important to do."

He and Susan locked glances again. This time, Bigelow couldn't miss what was going on.

"Susan!" he said. "Shall we continue or not?"

There was a long pause. Then Susan walked over and put her hand on Bigelow's arm.

"I'm sorry, Randy," she said softly. "I'm really not sure."

He took a few seconds to let this sink in. Then he removed her hand from his arm.

"Well, I *am!*" he said angrily. "Come on, Mother."

He turned and offered his arm to an outraged Mrs. Bigelow.

On the way up the aisle and out of the church, Bigelow slipped four more times. His mother caught him three times. The fourth time, he fell over backward and plopped down onto the floor.

Herbie sat at a curb near a phone booth. His roof was covered with Susan's luggage. The entire MacLane family was huddled inside, waiting for Jim to finish his call.

Jim hung up and got into the car. "Great news!" he said, starting Herbie up. "Bo got the entry fee back. Now all we have to do is get back home before he spends it!"

"You mean you're not even gonna *try* to make the race?" Robbie said, disappointed.

"Not now or ever," Susan said confidently.

"You heard the lady," Jim said, pulling out into traffic.

Matthew and Robbie both groaned. Then Julie did a great imitation of Randy Bigelow.

"There'll be no unhappy boys," she mimicked. "What is this, a wedding or a funeral?"

As they laughed at Julie's impersonation, a car passed them in the other lane. On its rear was a sign that read, JUST MARRIED.

" 'Here Comes the Bride'!" Herbie tooted.

Jim and Susan exchanged yet another glance. Julie happily caught this one, too.

Chapter 8 _____

Jim and Herbie spent the next few months getting to know the MacLane family. Jim took the boys on a couple of fishing trips. He doubled up on Julie's lessons, so that she passed her road test with flying colors. And he spent all the rest of his spare time with Susan.

There were a few rough spots, however. For one two-week period, Robbie wouldn't talk to anybody, except to complain about something or other. Susan and Jim were beginning to get pretty worried, when Robbie finally opened up.

He wasn't happy about all the time his

mother was spending out of the house. He missed all the attention Susan used to give her youngest child. What it came down to was that he was jealous of the new addition to the family—Jim Douglas.

When Jim found out what was wrong, he took Robbie for a long ride in the country. Having Herbie almost all to himself was just the thing Robbie needed. It loosened him up, and he told Jim what was on his mind.

Two hours—and a dozen reassurances—later, Jim and Robbie were as close as two pages in a book. By the time they got back home, Robbie couldn't even remember why they'd taken the trip.

Then there was the rough spot between Jim and Susan. Jim had asked her to marry him. Susan had said yes. Then they'd both stalled on just when the marriage should take place.

Jim's business was picking up, but he still wasn't sure he could afford to support five people. Susan wasn't going to force the issue, but she sometimes wondered if Jim wasn't just afraid of giving up his lifelong bachelorhood.

But the biggest—and most dangerous—rough spot of all was Randy Bigelow. He had spent the past few months trying to come up with a scheme that would destroy any plans Jim and Susan might have.

Bigelow sat in his office at the bank, his feet up on his desk, and his hands clasped behind his head. His mother knocked at the door and walked in.

"Thinking about how to increase the bank's business, dear?" she said.

"No, Mother. Actually, I was thinking of a way to save Susan from that demented race car driver."

"I don't want to hear that woman's name again!" Mrs. Bigelow said sharply. "She has caused me enough humilation—walking out in the middle of my wedding!"

"It was *my* wedding, Mother."

"I don't care!" she said. "It was *my* catering bill! Do you have any idea what it costs to ship one hundred fifty pounds of Maine lobster to California?"

"Well, Mother," Bigelow said, "I think I've come up with a way to bring Susan to her senses."

"Randy," she said patiently, "I'll make you a vice president and give you a raise of one hundred dollars a week. All you have to do is promise you'll never mention that woman's name to me again."

"They're not married yet, Mother," he said, getting up from his chair. "And if my plan works, they never will be."

A few miles away, Herbie puttered along a busy street, taking Jim from his home to the driving school. They came to a corner, and Jim began to turn left. Herbie turned right instead.

"Herbie!" Jim said. "Behave yourself! The school's the other way!"

Herbie's engine stalled, and he came to a stop.

"Stalling?" Jim said, amused. "For the third time this morning?"

He turned the ignition off, then on, and stepped on the accelerator. Herbie sputtered, but he wouldn't start up.

"Come on, Herbie. I know you're nervous about the wedding. But remember, *I'm* the one who's going to be at the altar, now that Susan and I have set the date."

He turned the key again and stepped on the accelerator. Herbie still wouldn't start.

"Okay, Herbie. I guess I'll have to put you in the shop. New plugs and points, adjust your carburetor, maybe a major tune-up. It'll probably take a few days, so you might miss the wedding."

That did it. Herbie started up, and they drove off down the street.

At the driving school, Bo stood at the curb, looking up and down the street. Suddenly, he spotted Herbie and called out, "Here they come!"

He ran back to join the other waiting people. As Herbie neared the school, Jim gasped in surprise.

The parking lot outside the office was filled with people. The driving school's sign had been decorated with banners, ribbons, and balloons. Over the window hung another sign that read, HAPPY WEDDING.

"Herbie," Jim said, "you sly old fox! *This* is why you were stalling!"

As Herbie pulled up, everyone cheered. Jim got out and walked into the middle of the crowd. Several people slapped him on the back or shook his hand.

Jason stepped up to him and said, "You want to get into my pool, Mr. Douglas? You pick a number—how many years you think the marriage will last."

"Or my pool," Raymond said, stepping up from behind. "Mine's in months."

"Thanks for your vote of confidence, gentlemen," Jim said, laughing.

Two of Jim's older women students stepped

forward and handed him a pair of pajamas. They were decorated with large red hearts on a white background.

"We picked the loudest pajamas we could find," Mrs. Furnstrom said, grinning.

"They're to keep you awake on your honeymoon," Mrs. Jessup added.

The loud laughter almost drowned out the voice of a man calling for attention. Then the voice became stronger, and everyone turned toward it.

"May I have your attention, please!" Randy Bigelow was calling. "Attention, everybody! I have something to say!"

Bigelow was standing at the curb, next to Herbie's rear wheels. The guests quieted down and faced him.

"Thank you," he said.

Herbie gave a good squirt of oil to Bigelow's pants and shoes. The crowd laughed again, and Bigelow looked down angrily at the mess. Then he looked up and forced a big smile.

"The first thing is, I wish someone would fix the oil leak on this . . . this *adorable* little car."

He carefully stepped out of the oil puddle and walked up to Jim.

"But I'm really here to say something to

you, Jim," he said smiling sweetly. "As you know, I had plans for Susan myself. But . . . the better man won. No hard feelings." He looked down at his messy pants and shoes. "About anything," he added.

Everyone cheered. Jim stepped forward, and the two men shook hands.

"WHONNNNK!" Herbie said, and Bigelow jumped in surprise.

"Er, Randy," Jim said quickly, trying to cover Herbie's remark, "and everyone else, too. Herbie and I are grateful. Susan will be, too. This is a wonderful show of generosity from you, my students and friends. There seems to be only one thing to say to such a fine group." His eyes twinkled mischievously. "That is, *when two cars approach an intersection at the same time, the right-of-way belongs to—*"

The rest of his announcement was drowned out by a friendly chorus of boos and catcalls. Smiling even more broadly than everyone else, Bigelow backed away from the crowd toward a potted plant next to the office.

This was the real reason he was here. He wanted to check on the microphone his private detective had hidden in the plant. There it was, a tiny bugging device that would supply him with what he needed. He slinked away and headed back to the bank.

The day before the wedding, Susan's house was in a state of near-chaos. She and the kids were moving clothes from one closet to another . . . to another . . . to another. The idea was to somehow make room for Jim's stuff. It wasn't working out very well.

Susan stepped into Matthew's and Robbie's room with an armload of dresses on hangers. When they saw her, they rushed in front of the closet door and blocked her way.

"Sorry, Mom," Robbie said. "No ladies' clothes in our closet."

"Step aside," Susan said wearily. "You have plenty of room in there."

"We took a vote," Matthew said. "You lost two to nothing."

"Well, count again," Susan said. "I win four to two."

"Four?!" Matthew and Robbie said together.

"That's right," Susan said, pointing to herself with her free hand. "Mother, cook, housekeeper, and senior officer."

Julie stepped in from the hall and said, "You forgot 'nervous bride.' "

"And getting more nervous by the minute," Susan said, struggling her way past her two defeated sons.

"Why can't Jim just move into the attic?" Robbie asked, slumping on the floor. Susan smiled at Robbie's question. "No wonder the poor man's nervous about getting married," she said, hanging her dresses in the boys' closet.

"Oh, I don't know, Mom," Julie said. "Jim doesn't seem very nervous to me."

"He will be by the time he gets to this madhouse," Susan said.

"I've never seen anybody so nervous in all my life," Bo said. He was in Jim's apartment, helping him stuff everything he owned into a collection of suitcases and paper cartons.

"Me, neither," Jim said. "And you're only the best man!"

They bent down together to pick up the pieces of a vase Bo had just dropped.

"Sorry," Bo said. "Maybe *you* should handle all this stuff. *I'll* just sit on the sidelines and direct."

"Good," Jim said grinning. "That way, the groom won't have to worry about the best man's nerves."

"Right," Bo said. He began to pace back and forth, as Jim calmly continued packing his things.

"Because I don't want you to have to worry about anything," Bo added.

"I feel great, Bo. No kidding. I'm happy. I'm doing just what I want to do."

"Yeah, yeah," Bo said nervously. "And if you're the least bit worried, just tell old Big Daddy Bo. That's what I'm here for. And to get you to the church tomorrow."

He picked up the speed of his pacing. Jim was only half-listening as Bo continued to babble on.

"Because there's no wedding without the groom, the bride, and the ring. And *you* have the bride. And the *bride* has you." He stopped pacing and stared at the wall. "Now, *who* has the ring?"

"I gave you the ring yesterday," Jim said, as he closed the top on the carton he'd just filled.

"*I've* got the ring?" Bo shrieked. "I *haven't* got the ring! I'd better find the ring!"

Jim stopped working. He laughed as Bo went into a panic, looking through his pockets, under a chair, along the floor.

"I *am* nervous!" Bo said, searching. "But

you *should* be! No ring! Can't have a wedding without a ring!"

Suddenly, he stopped and reacted in surprise. He was staring at his own right hand. There, on his pinky, was the wedding ring.

"I've got it!" he cried, deliriously happy. "I've got it! I told you there was nothing to worry about!"

Jim went back to his packing. Bo fell into a chair, breathing heavily, a look of relief on his face.

"Everything's okay," he sighed. "There'll be smooth sailing from now on."

Bo rested his arm on a small table. The table stood in front of a heating vent in the lower part of a wall.

Neither Bo nor Jim would have had any reason to look inside that vent. But if they had looked, they'd have seen something very curious.

A tiny microphone was taped to the bottom part of the grill. It was picking up everything they said.

It was exactly the same as the microphone in the potted plant outside the driving school office. And it had been planted by the same private detective, for the same reason.

Randy Bigelow was recording Jim's private conversations.

When Herbie and Jim Douglas (Dean Jones) catch the
bank robbers, they also save the thieves' pretty hostage,
Susan MacLane (Patricia Harty).

Jim and Susan introduce themselves. Jim learns that Susan is the mother of Julie MacLane, one of his driving students at the high school. Susan asks Jim to give her daughter private driving lessons.

Julie (Claudia Wells) is embarrassed when fellow students Jason (Bryan Utman) and Raymond (Kipp Lennon) tease her for driving Herbie — Jim's "late model" instruction car.

Herbie nudges
Bigelow's flashy
convertible into a
row of sprinklers.

(*Below*): Bigelow
(Larry Linville)
wants revenge. He
slips into Herbie
and steers him
straight for a line
of garbage cans.

But it's *Herbie*
who dumps
Bigelow among
the orange peels.

"Herbie no longer has what it takes to race," taunt Jim's students. But that afternoon, Herbie can't resist racing them, and proving the boys wrong — with Jim and Susan as unwilling passengers.

Angry at being "dragged" to the drag strip by Jim and Herbie, Susan decides to marry Bigelow. But Julie doesn't trust Bigelow. Is her mother making a mistake?

Herbie makes up for his foolish clowning at the drag strip by whisking Jim off to Susan's and Bigelow's wedding — just in time to stop the ceremony.

Susan calls off her marriage to Bigelow, and Jim begins to spend more time with the MacLane family. Here, Jim takes Matthew (Nicky Katt) and Robbie (Douglas Emerson) fishing.

Meanwhile, Bigelow plots with Rainey (Lee Paul) to get rid of Herbie for good.

Herbie shakes with fear as the giant forklift lowers him into the compactor . . .

Jim arrives at the wrecking yard just in time to save Herbie.

Jim and Susan exchange marriage vows, as the MacLane kids look on. After the ceremony, Julie, Matthew, and Robbie cheer, while Herbie toots "Here Comes the Bride"!

Chapter 9 _____

Sitting in his office, Bigelow held the two tiny microphones in his hand. He gently tossed them up and down as he spoke.

"These are very interesting, O'Brien," Bigelow said. "But I'm not really interested in your machinery. All I care about is what you found out with these things."

"Depends on what you're looking for," O'Brien said, taking the mikes from him.

O'Brien was a short, squat man who wore a rumpled suit and chewed on an unlit cigar. He needed a shave, his shirt was wrinkled, and his tie was crooked. In general, he was rather a seedy character.

"What I'm looking for," Bigelow said, "is

something to ruin Jim Douglas. This man broke up my wedding. And I intend to return the favor. At the last minute, if possible, just as he did."

"Well," O'Brien said, shaking his head, "I'm not sure I'm gonna be able to help you. I've bugged car thieves, embezzlers, forgers, con men—"

"I don't need your resumé!" Bigelow fumed. "I got that before I hired you. What about Jim Douglas?"

"Clean," O'Brien said, shifting the cigar to the other side of his mouth. "Stays out of trouble. Doesn't smoke. Doesn't drink. Doesn't go out with other women. You couldn't even get him to do a beer commercial."

"Never mind what he would or wouldn't *do*! What has he *done*?"

"I bugged him," O'Brien said. "I tapped his phone. I tailed him for a week. Believe me, I couldn't find a thing. Never seen anybody so clean. Wish my daughter would bring home a guy like him. Instead of those bums she's been hanging around with."

"I don't care about your daughter!" Bigelow roared. "What am I paying you for?"

"I did what you paid me for, Bigelow. I

can't find what isn't there," O'Brien said firmly.

"Well, I'm going to get him anyway," Bigelow vowed, his eyes narrowing and his face turning red. "I'll get him with or without you! But I . . . will . . . get . . . him!"

Susan was lining an empty dresser drawer with paper when she heard Jim's voice.

"Honey? You in there?"

"Yeah. In the bedroom," she called.

When he came in, she left the drawer and gave him a hug and a kiss. Then she got back to work.

"Where are your things?" Susan asked.

"Home," Jim said, as he dropped into a big, overstuffed chair.

"Home? I thought you were going to bring them over today."

"Well, I heard Robbie and Matthew complaining last night. I wasn't sure it was definite."

"What . . . about tomorrow?" she asked, facing him.

"Tomorrow?" he said, laughing. "Oh, tomorrow is definitely definite!"

Susan studied him for a moment, wondering if his laughter hadn't been a little forced.

"Sorry," she said. "But I guess I'm a little surprised. I made room in the closet, cleared out a few drawers."

"But they'll still be available after the honeymoon, won't they?" Jim asked.

"Of course," Susan replied. Then she raised an eyebrow and asked, "Will you?"

"Susan," Jim said, "what's wrong? We agreed that I'd move in here because there's more room in the house for the kids. This *is* where we'll be living, isn't it?"

"I thought so. But I also thought you were going to move in today. Unless you still have doubts about moving in at all."

"I don't have any doubts about anything!" Jim said, raising his voice slightly. "Why doesn't anybody believe me when I say that?"

"Because," Susan said, "it just isn't normal for a man to be this casual the day before his wedding!"

Jim was getting angry. "I just thought it could wait until after the honeymoon, that's all," he said.

Susan wasn't satisfied. "Well, it sounds like an excuse for putting things off," she said hotly.

Outside the house, Herbie sat at the curb

with his antenna up. It was pointed toward the bedroom window, and he was picking up the whole conversation. Or was it an argument?

Herbie wasn't going to wait to find out. He pulled away from the curb and hurried to a gas station a few blocks away.

In one section of the gas station was a collection of small trailers—the kind people use to move personal belongings. Herbie backed into this section and eased toward the connecting rod of one of the trailers.

Ten minutes later, he pulled up in front of Jim's apartment house. He honked his horn, and Bo popped his head out of the window. A couple of minutes later, Bo came down, carrying two cartons.

"I thought you'd be back, Jim," Bo said. "Changed your mind about moving today, huh?"

He put the cartons down and looked around. "Jim? Where are you?"

Bo looked up and down the street. Jim was not in sight. Bo picked up the cartons and put them in the trailer. "Where does it say the groom ducks out and leaves all the work to the best man?" he said.

Bo stepped back and looked at Herbie. Then he blinked a few times.

"What am I talking to *you* for? I'm getting as crazy as Jim!"

He turned and went back upstairs for another load.

Jim and Susan sat on the couch in the living room. Susan's friend, Elizabeth, sat across from them, spreading several travel folders out on the coffee table.

"Don't worry, you two," Elizabeth said reassuringly. "I'm a whiz at making last-minute reservations."

"Isn't it great to have a travel agent for a friend?" Susan said to Jim.

Elizabeth went on. "Now, I can get you a beautiful room overlooking the ocean, or maybe you'd like to be further up the coast. There's this charming hotel right on a cliff. The food is only so-so, but the view is *spectacular*. Of course, there's always the desert. I know a great spot with a pool and a health spa."

Jim looked from one folder to another. Then he looked up at Elizabeth.

"I just don't know," he said helplessly. "So many choices."

"Maybe we can decide after the honeymoon," Susan teased.

"Honey," Jim said, "this *is* the honeymoon."

Then he realized he was being kidded. "Oh, I see," he said. "This is still the when-are-you-moving-in question."

Susan glanced toward the window and looked surprised. Then she smiled at Jim and playfully slapped him on the arm.

"You pulled a fast one on me!" she said, grinning.

Jim and Elizabeth exchanged confused glances. Then Susan pointed out the window.

"Your things were here all the time, weren't they?" she said to Jim.

Jim looked out and saw Herbie and the loaded trailer. He rolled his eyes toward heaven, then turned back with a sheepish grin.

"Well . . . I . . . uh . . ."

"I never know when he's kidding me," Susan said to Elizabeth.

"Sometimes I'm not sure myself," Jim added.

"Listen, you two," Elizabeth said, standing up and heading for the door. "Pick a place for your honeymoon. But let me know soon. And I mean in an hour or so."

After she'd left, Jim said, "I'd better unload that stuff, before it unloads itself."

"Wait," Susan said. "I want to show you something."

She went to the hall closet and brought out a large box. She opened it to reveal a very old—and very elegant—wedding dress.

"It's the gown my grandmother wore at her wedding, Jim. I'd like to wear it tomorrow."

"It would look lovely on you," Jim said hesitantly. "But . . . doesn't it need to be fitted or something? Or did you wear it at your first . . . uh . . ."

"Yes, Jim, I did. And if you don't want me to wear it at our wedding . . ."

"No, no. It's all right," Jim said.

Susan pulled the bottom part of the dress out of the box. A large tear ran down the front.

"Maybe I've been worried about nothing," she said sadly.

"Sorry, honey," Jim said lightly. "Looks like a pretty bad tear. And I'm useless with a needle and thread."

He smiled and went out to the car. She stared after him, wondering why he had joked about the gown.

"Drivel!" Bigelow sputtered. "Hours and hours of drivel!"

He was at his desk, wearing a headset. He'd spent the last three hours listening to the tapes that O'Brien had left with him. His mother came in to hear the tail end of his complaint, as he threw the headset angrily on the desk.

"Douglas is so clean, he's boring!"

"When you carry on like this," his mother said calmly, "you're as boring as he is. Why don't you get him out of your mind, Randell?"

"Mother!" he said in astonishment. "How can you say a thing like that to me? You know the closest thing to my heart is revenge!"

"I'm warning you, Randell," she said. "If you keep this up, you're going to be sick again."

"I don't care!" he said, pounding his fists on his desk. "As long as I get Douglas and that ridiculous little car of his! Now leave me alone! I have to think!"

Bigelow loosened his tie and began to pace across the floor of his office. His mother stood to one side, watching him walk nervously back and forth.

"I just don't like to see you this way," Mrs. Bigelow said. "It reminds me of when you were in high school. Remember when you imagined that those boys were out to get you?"

Bigelow stopped pacing and turned to her.

"They were!" he yelled. "They *were* out to get me! And all because I had the only sports car in the twelfth grade! And you know what they did to me, Mother? They ruined my graduation! They put that horrible stink bomb in my beautiful car, and—"

He stopped suddenly, and his eyes lit up. His face melted into an angelic smile.

"Mother," he said softly, "I love you." He kissed her cheek and said, "I love you, Mother."

Then he fell back into his chair, smiling into space.

"Randell," Mrs. Bigelow said, frowning. "Randell, dear, are you all right?"

"Mother," he said, rubbing his hands, "I have never been so all right in my entire life!"

Chapter 10 _____

Bigelow pulled his car to a stop in front of a large, peeling sign. RAINEY'S WRECKING YARD, it said.

On one side of the large yard was a meat-packing plant. On the other side was a run-down, deserted warehouse. Bigelow parked his car in front of the warehouse and walked back to the yard's entrance gate.

He stepped through the gate and found himself surrounded by broken-down cars and rusty car parts. Tires, wheels, and emptied-out auto bodies were scattered all over the ground.

There was a shack in the middle of the yard, and Bigelow assumed this was the "office." Carefully, he made his way in that direction, feeling as though he were walking through a graveyard.

As he approached the shack, a man opened the door and stepped out. He was huge, well over six feet tall, and probably well over two hundred fifty pounds, too. He looked strong enough to crush one of the cars in his yard with his bare hands.

The man stood leaning in the doorway as Bigelow approached. Bigelow stopped a few feet from him, not wanting to get too close.

"Yeah?" the man growled. "Help ya?"

"I'm looking for a Mr. . . ." Bigelow took a card from his pocket and looked at it.

"Rainey," the man said. "You found him."

"Oh, good!" Bigelow said, a little too cheerfully. "My name is Bigelow."

He started to extend his hand to Rainey. Then he thought better of it.

"Yeah?" Rainey growled again.

"You were . . . uh . . . referred to me," Bigelow said, "by a private detective." The last part of the sentence was almost whispered.

When Rainey didn't react, Bigelow added, "His name's O'Brien."

Rainey's face finally showed some signs

that he was human. "Oh, yeah," he said. "O'Brien. I used to go out with his daughter."

"Well, he said you could . . . that is, you might be willing to . . ."

"What is it? You got a hot car?"

"No, no," Bigelow said. "Nothing like that. It's just that . . . well . . . I'd like you to do something for me. And O'Brien said you were the kind of man who didn't ask a lot of questions."

"I only ask one question," Rainey said, stepping toward him. "You got bucks?"

Bigelow took a few steps back to keep some distance between them. Then he took out a wallet filled with cash. Rainey stared at the bills.

"Whatta ya want done?" he asked.

Bigelow took a deep breath, then blurted it out. "I want a stink bomb put in a car."

"A stink bomb?!" Rainey said.

"No questions," Bigelow reminded him.

Rainey shrugged his shoulders. "No questions," he said.

"Now, I want it to go off at a particular time tomorrow. I'll deliver the car. You deliver the stink bomb."

Rainey looked from Bigelow to his wallet and back again. "You got it," he said.

*　　　*　　　*

An hour later, Jim, Susan, and the three kids stood in a small chapel, waiting for instructions from Reverend Talbot. The minister held several loose papers and a prayer book, which he kept thumbing through nervously.

"A rehearsal is usually a good idea," he was saying. "It can help calm the nerves. We get acquainted, and we know exactly what's going to happen tomorrow. That way, there won't be any slip-ups."

As he said the last part, he dropped the book and papers. Jim quickly bent down to help him retrieve them.

Some of the papers fluttered away, and Robbie and Matthew joined in. When everything had been recovered, the minister spoke again.

"Thank you, thank you." He turned to Julie. "Now, you're the bride?"

"No," Susan said. "She's my daughter. I'm the bride."

"Oh, of course, of course," Reverend Talbot said nervously. "I'm terribly sorry. No offense meant. And, I hope, no offense taken. Now, where's the best man?"

"That's Bo," Jim said. "But one of us had to work this afternoon. Under the circumstances, I figured it should be him."

"I was best man in a play at school!" Matthew said.

"Oh, good!" Reverend Talbot sang.

"It was a mystery," Matthew explained. "I poisoned the groom!"

Jim gave him a curious look, as Reverend Talbot asked, "And we also have a matron of honor?"

"She's our travel agent," Susan said. "If she doesn't work today, we don't have a honeymoon tomorrow."

"I can fill in for her," Julie offered, smiling, "since you won't let me be the bride."

"Will there be a flower girl?" the minister asked. He was looking at Robbie as he spoke.

"Not me!" Robbie said. "I don't even want her clothes in my closet!"

Smiling, Reverend Talbot said, "Well, why don't we all get in position, then?"

Somehow, his prayer book and papers fell to the floor again. This time everyone bent down to pick things up. Jim and Susan found themselves head-to-head.

"Maybe we should hold the ceremony down here," he whispered to her.

Bigelow's sports car pulled up across the street from the chapel entrance. He eyed

Herbie maliciously. Miss Schaefer, his secretary, sat in the passenger seat next to him.

"Do you want me to wait, Mr. Bigelow?" she asked.

"I don't need anyone around while I'm 'borrowing' a car, Miss Schaefer."

"If you'll excuse me, sir," she said, as he got out. "You have such a nice car here. I can't think of why you'd borrow a funny little car like that one."

"That's none of your business, Miss Schaefer," he said, as she slid into the driver's seat. "Now, go! I'm in a hurry."

When Miss Schaefer had driven off, Bigelow walked across the street to Herbie. After checking to see that no one was around, he slipped into the driver's seat. Then he bent over and proceeded to hotwire the car.

"Douglas," he said, as he strained under the steering wheel, "you are in for one big surprise."

Herbie started up. Bigelow straightened and pulled away from the curb. He chuckled evily as they turned a corner.

Two blocks from the chapel, Herbie and Bigelow approached a police car. Two policemen sat inside, watching the traffic.

As they passed the patrol car, Herbie veered sharply to the right. Bigelow gripped the wheel and pulled in the opposite direction.

Herbie went with the tug and veered left. Then right, left, and right again.

"What's wrong with this steering wheel?" Bigelow yelled.

The patrol car pulled out and took off after Herbie. He was doing a left-right dance now, forcing cars to pull over and pedestrians to run for cover.

The policemen turned on their siren and their flashing red lights.

Herbie picked up speed and continued veering from side to side. He was careful not to go too fast, since he had every intention of being overtaken by the police.

They caught up with him in a matter of seconds. Then they were slightly ahead of him, forcing him to pull over to the curb. Bigelow was still trying to get control of the wheel, with no success. When Herbie finally stopped, Bigelow felt as though he'd come to the end of a high-speed roller-coaster ride.

A policeman walked up to Bigelow's window. Bigelow was blinking crazily, trying to fight the dizziness.

"It's okay, officer," he said. "Just something wrong with the steering."

"Step out, please," the policeman said.

"Officer, I'm in kind of a hurry!"

"So are we," the policeman said, opening the door. As he did, Bigelow fell out on the ground. The second policeman helped him to his feet.

"Any more rough stuff like that," Bigelow said, pulling away from the policeman, "and I'll have your badges!"

"You can have them, Rubber Legs," the first officer said. "Right after you pass the sobriety test."

"Drinking?" Bigelow said, reeling from side to side. "You think I've been drinking?!"

"Our first clue," the policeman said, "was the way you performed those figure eights."

"I am cold sober!" Bigelow protested. "I am a bank officer and an honorary member of the Marine Color Guard!"

"You'd better come downtown with us," the policeman said quietly.

"Never, never, never!"

Bigelow might have said it a dozen more times. But he noticed the second officer sliding his hand toward his gun holster.

"Will it take very long, Officer?" he asked meekly.

As they pulled away, Herbie quietly made

a U-turn and returned to the chapel.

Susan was kneeling on the floor of the hall closet, tossing things out over her shoulder. Julie came down the stairs.

"Lose something, Mom?"

"Have you seen Grandma's wedding dress?"

"No," Julie said. "I thought you put it away."

"I was just going to," Susan said, standing. "I thought I'd left it here."

"I haven't seen it," Julie shrugged.

"Come to think of it, I haven't either," Susan said. "Not since I showed it to Jim earlier today. You don't suppose he . . ."

"He what?" Julie asked, mystified.

"Well," Susan considered, "he didn't seem too anxious for me to wear it."

"Did he say that?"

"No, but I could tell by what he didn't say. I'm not sure what he had against it. He just seemed—not very excited about my wearing it. I just wish he'd had a little more faith in me. I wouldn't have considered wearing it if he objected. He didn't have to take it away!"

"Mother," Julie said, "you don't know that he did."

"Well, then where is it?!"

"Never!" Mrs. Bigelow said. "I have never been so humiliated in my life!"

She stomped down the steps leading from the police station, her son tagging along after her.

"And I will never go through this kind of humiliation again!" she added.

"*You?*" Bigelow said, catching up with her. "What about *me*? I wasn't even drinking!"

"You must be a throwback to your great-grandfather!" she said. "On your father's side!"

"Mother, it was that car! There is something very strange about that infernal car!"

She stopped walking and turned to face him. She looked straight into his eyes.

"Son," she said, "when a person is sick, he really shouldn't drink."

"I wasn't drinking, Mother!" he pleaded. "Why does that car treat me this way? I've seen those little old ladies driving it. It's so nicey-nicey, butter wouldn't melt in its mouth!"

"Your great-grandfather was a disgrace to the Bigelow name," she said.

But he wasn't listening. His face was lit up

again with that same angelic grin he'd had in his office.

"Little old ladies? . . ." he said.

"Randell? What is it now?"

"Mother!" he said, kissing her on the cheek. "Mother, I love you!" He turned and ran off.

Mrs. Bigelow called after him. "The last two years of your great-grandfather's life, he couldn't even have visitors!"

But it was no use. He was gone. She shook her head sadly and walked to her car.

Chapter 11 _____

Herbie pulled up in front of a row of small stores. Jim got out, reached inside, and took out a large box. It was the same box Susan had been looking for in her closet. He carried it into one of the stores.

As soon as he was gone, the sports car pulled up a few spaces behind Herbie. Miss Schaefer was driving this time. An old lady sat next to her in the passenger seat.

"Here we are," Miss Schaefer said. "You want me to wait this time, Mr. Bigelow?"

"Not *Mr. Bigelow!*" he hissed. "*Auntie!* You must have an old auntie in your family!"

"Not one who looks like you."

"Then fake it!" he said. "People are looking at us. Kiss Auntie good-bye."

"You pay me a good salary, Mr. Bigelow," Miss Schaefer said. "But you don't pay me enough for that!"

He glared at her from under his wig. Then he opened the door and began to slowly climb out of the car.

"Are you sure you don't want me to wait around?" Miss Schaefer asked. "I've had nurse's training, you know," she added sarcastically.

"Get moving!" he said through his teeth.

She pulled away, and he stood there in his old lady's outfit, leaning on his cane. Then slowly, very slowly, he made his way down the street to Herbie.

Bigelow reached the car and smiled his old lady smile at it. Then he patted it on the hood affectionately. He walked around to the driver's side and got in. Herbie started right up for him.

"Now, let's see," he said in a high-pitched voice, "where is that nasty old first gear?"

He shifted into first gear. His eyes narrowed. *The plan was going to work!*

"Now we're going to take a nice little ride with *Auntie*," he said.

Herbie pulled away from the space. Bigelow sat hunched over the wheel, the way he thought an old lady might. As Herbie moved along, Bigelow sang a little tune in his best old lady voice.

He cackled gleefully when they passed the same patrol car that had given him trouble earlier. But he stopped cackling when Herbie began to lurch and buck down the street.

"Stop that!" Bigelow said in his own deep voice. He pounded on the steering wheel and screamed, "Stop that, you miserable little runt!"

Herbie lurched and bucked, going nowhere. He looked like a mechanical bull in a rodeo. The jolts sent Bigelow flying forward and backward. When the policemen reached his car, his wig was over the front of his face.

"What do we have here?" the first officer asked, as Herbie quieted down.

"Same car," his partner said. "Different driver."

"Or is it?" the first officer said, reaching in through the window and fingering the wig. "Would you mind stepping out . . . uh . . . madam?"

"Have you no respect for senior citizens?" Bigelow said, his old lady voice back again.

"Not when they drive like you do," the policeman said, opening the door.

Bigelow climbed out of the car. "I know what you're thinking," he said.

"Step over to the curb," the policeman said. He closed the door, and Bigelow's wide skirt got caught inside.

"I assure you I have *not* been drinking," Bigelow said, taking a step toward the curb.

As he did, the skirt ripped off and revealed his bare, boney legs.

"What *have* you been doing?" the policeman asked, smiling.

Jim stood in his apartment, holding a dark blue suit, just back from the dry cleaner's. He went to answer a knock at the door. He was startled to see Susan standing in the hall.

"Hi, honey!" he said. "This is a nice surprise."

"You busy?" she asked, stepping inside.

"No," he said, closing the door behind her. "Just a few last-minute things. I just picked this suit up from the cleaner's. Wish it looked as good on me as it does on the hanger."

Without smiling, Susan asked, "Don't you wonder what *I'm* going to be wearing?"

"Well, yeah . . . " Jim said uncomfortably.

"Or is it that you know what I'm *not* going to be wearing," she said.

Jim looked puzzled. "I think I missed a turn somewhere," he said.

"I know we have a lifetime to get to know each other," she said, walking around the room. "But I want to be open about what's on my mind."

"Fine," Jim said, with no idea of what she was getting at.

"I wish you'd been open with me this morning, Jim. About the dress."

Jim looked at her curiously. Did she know? How could she?

"If you didn't want me to wear it," she went on, still pacing, "why didn't you just say so? Instead of taking it."

She stopped and faced him. "That is, if you did take it."

Then her eye was caught by something on the floor. She walked over to it angrily.

"And you *did*!" she said triumphantly.

Jim watched as she bent to open the box. There was her dress. But she was a little surprised to see it wrapped in tissue paper. She picked up a card taped to the paper.

She read the card out loud. "Grandma

would have loved to see you in her dress. And so would I."

She turned to Jim, with tears in her eyes. While she was still unable to speak, he did.

"Surprise, honey," he said softly.

"Jim," she said. "Thank you." She put her arms around his neck and gave him a big kiss.

A few minutes after midnight, Herbie sat at the curb outside the apartment house. Except for a gentle breeze rustling the leaves of the trees, the street was silent.

Then another sound disturbed the peace. It was a tow truck coming around the corner. It pulled up in front of Herbie, with Bigelow, in his sports car, close behind.

As Bigelow watched, two men got out of the tow truck. One of them carried a large sheet of canvas. Together, they spread the canvas out and covered Herbie with it.

In less than two minutes, the two men had hooked their tow line to Herbie's front end. Then they got back in the truck and pulled away, dragging Herbie behind them.

Bigelow rubbed his hands together and chuckled. Then he followed the tow truck to the wrecking yard.

Rainey was waiting for them with his tool box. The tow truck pulled Herbie into the yard. The two men got out and unhooked their line.

Bigelow took out his wallet. He handed a fifty-dollar bill to each of the men. Then they got into the truck and drove away.

Bigelow watched Rainey take a long, flat tool from his tool box and go into action. He slipped the tool into the tiny space where the door met the frame. He jimmied it back and forth. Nothing happened.

Bigelow looked at his watch impatiently. Rainey tried another tool. Again, nothing happened. He tried a third tool, with the same results.

Annoyed, Bigelow said, "I thought you were an expert at this!"

Rainey stepped back and wiped the sweat from his forehead. "I never seen a car door I couldn't pick open," he said in wonder.

"You've never seen a car like *this* one before," Bigelow said.

"I can't spend all night here," Rainey said. "You want a stink bomb in there, I'm gonna have to break a window."

"No, no, no! It has to look exactly as it does now! There *must* be another way."

Rainey watched him as he began walking

in circles, trying to decide what to do. Suddenly, Bigelow stopped and stared wide-eyed at something behind Rainey.

"There *is* another way!" he said, pointing.

Rainey turned to see what Bigelow was staring at. There, in a corner of the yard, sat another VW bug. It was light green. But, other than that, it looked exactly like Herbie.

"There!" Bigelow said excitedly, pointing to the green car. "What would it take to paint that one so it looks like *this* one?"

Rainey looked from the green car to Herbie. Then he held out his hand.

Bigelow reached for his wallet and said, "By tomorrow morning."

Rainey nodded. Bigelow began counting out several bills from his wallet.

Chapter 12 _____

Bo rang Jim's bell, waited three seconds, then knocked on the door. Then he rang and knocked again.

The door opened, and Jim stood inside, wearing a bathrobe and rubbing his eyes. Bo stepped past him into the apartment.

"Look at you!" Bo bubbled. "Not even up yet!"

Jim closed the door, looked at his watch, and turned around very slowly.

"It's three hours till the wedding," he said, rubbing the back of his neck.

"I know," Bo said. "But I couldn't sleep. I guess I'm a little nervous."

Jim walked over to the kitchen area and

began making coffee. "What are you so nervous about?" he yawned.

"You!" Bo exploded. "You're so calm, you're making me nervous!"

"Sit down and relax," Jim said lazily. "This is my one-in-a-million morning. I don't want anything to spoil it."

"Of course," Bo said, "I know it's all an act. I noticed that Herbie wasn't in his usual spot. What happened? You couldn't sleep last night, I bet. Had to take a drive, right?"

"I slept like a baby," Jim laughed. "And Herbie is right where he belongs. Now take it easy, will you?"

Herbie, of course, wasn't anywhere near where he belonged. He was several miles away, in the wrecking yard with Randy Bigelow and Mr. Rainey.

"Perfect!" Bigelow said. "It's an absolutely perfect copy!"

The two Volkswagens stood side-by-side. The light green one had been painted the same color as Herbie.

"So perfect," Rainey said, "I can't remember which is which."

"That's easy to find out," Bigelow said.

He stepped up to one of the cars and kicked the bumper. Nothing happened.

Then he went to the other car and kicked the bumper. A squirt of oil covered his cuff and his shoe.

"Here's the dirty little original!" he said angrily.

Rainey pointed to the other car. "Then that's the one with the stink bomb," he said.

"How is it set up?"

"There's a switch on the outside of the case," Rainey said. "Throw the switch after you park the car. The bomb will go off when the car has been moving for five minutes."

"Oh, beautiful!" Bigelow sang out.

"What happens to this one?" Rainey asked, pointing to Herbie.

Bigelow was aware of a loud, unpleasant noise that had been growing for the past few seconds. He turned to see a huge forklift lowering its clamps on the wreck of a car.

He watched in awe as the forklift picked the car up and swung it around in a semicircle. The car now hung over an enormous open-topped machine.

The clamps opened out, and the car fell into the machine. The crunching of glass and metal now drowned out every other sound.

"What do you call that machine?" Bigelow asked, grinning.

114

"Compactor," Rainey said.

"Well, *that*," Bigelow said triumphantly, "is what happens to this one!" He kicked Herbie's bumper and quickly hopped out of the way of the oil squirt.

"It's your money," Rainey said, shrugging his shoulders.

"Yes, it is," Bigelow said. "And because it's my money, I have one other demand to make. I want the job done exactly at noon!"

"Whatever you say."

"What wonderful timing!" Bigelow ranted. "Not only will the wedding be ruined! But this . . . this *car* . . . will suffer death by crunching at precisely the same moment!"

Bigelow got the imitation car into Herbie's space with plenty of time to spare. Then he got into his own car and drove to the chapel. Susan and the kids were already there, with Elizabeth.

"Radiant!" Bigelow said, as he walked up to the bride. "You look radiant, Susan!"

"You do," Elizabeth added. "So what else is new?"

"Thanks," Susan said, smiling. "Let's assume I make it through the wedding. Where am I going for a honeymoon?"

Elizabeth's face lit up. "A gorgeous suite overlooking the ocean!"

"How did you manage that?" Susan asked.

"Last-minute cancellation. Some poor groom got cold feet."

"Where is *our* groom?" Bigelow chirped. "I'm nearly as nervous as I was on my almost wedding."

"He'll be here," Susan said, straightening the folds of her wedding dress.

Jim and Bo came out of the apartment house together. Bo spotted the VW in its usual space, then shook his head in confusion.

"Right where I left him," Jim said.

"Yeah," Bo said. "Well, I did my best to make you nervous. The rest is up to you."

Jim laughed. "See you in church," he called, as Bo went to his own car.

Bo pulled away, and Jim climbed into the imposter. "A big day, Herbie," he said.

He started the car and pulled away. "You know where we're going, don't you? Let me give you a hint."

He whistled the first four notes of "Here Comes the Bride."

"You honked that so many times, I was beginning to think you wrote it." Jim stopped for a red light.

"Funny," he said. "I would have expected

you to be playing it all over town this morning."

"Hope you're not having second thoughts," he continued, as the light changed. "Because I'm not." He frowned and slapped himself on the forehead.

"I know! You're sulking!" Jim cried. "You're annoyed because you're not going on the honeymoon!"

They were approaching the business district now. A patrol car was parked a few blocks ahead of them. Inside were the two policemen who had nabbed Bigelow when he was trying to kidnap Herbie.

"Well, sulk away," Jim said cheerfully. "This is a honeymoon for *two*."

He looked over at the seat next to his. "Even if you do have new upholstery for the occasion," he said, smiling.

He looked back at the road, then did a double take to the seat.

"New upholstery?!"

He turned around to look at the back seat. As he did, the car swerved sharply to the right. It was heading straight for the police car.

Jim turned back in time to see what was about to happen. "Herbie!" he shouted.

Too late. They sideswiped the police car. Jim grabbed the wheel, got control of "Herbie," and pulled to a stop.

The police car was heading toward them. Jim jumped out of the car and looked at his right fender.

"Your first accident, Herbie!" he said. "And you had to pick a police car! Now we're going to be late for the wedding!"

The police car pulled up behind "Herbie," and the two officers got out. Jim stood shaking his head at the dented fender.

"Nice work," he muttered, as the policemen walked toward him.

"Right down to the green paint," Jim said absently. Then his eyes widened, and he said loudly, *"Green paint?"*

"May I see your driver's license, please?" the policeman asked.

"Herbie never had any green paint on him!" Jim said in response. "Officer, I thought this was Herbie, but Herbie was never painted green in his life! I know him as well as I know myself!"

"I think we have another one," one officer said to the other.

"Herbie!" Jim explained. "That's what I call my car!"

"Your car?" one of the policemen said.

"Where's the drunk and the little old lady?"

"I don't know what you're talking about," Jim said desperately. "I own this car. Or one just like it. But this isn't my car! The question is, where *is* my car?"

The policemen exchanged another glance.

"Would you mind if I call the chapel?" Jim asked.

"You won't get any help from there," the policeman said.

"I know you think I'm loony," Jim said, back in control of himself. "But I'm supposed to get married in fifteen minutes. I want to call my bride and tell her what's going on here."

At that moment, Herbie was being towed in the direction of the crusher. He locked his wheels, so they wouldn't spin. But the truck was too strong for him. His tires screeched as the truck dragged him along.

Herbie was pulled into a line of cars. Three other cars stood between him and the compactor.

Herbie began to backfire in protest. No one in the yard paid the slightest attention to the sounds.

"I'm fine," Jim said into the phone, as the

119

policemen listened. "But somebody has taken Herbie. I've been driving a car that's been painted to look like him!"

"You're finally sounding like the nervous groom," Susan laughed. "Tell me where you are. We'll send someone over to pick you up."

"But I have to find Herbie!"

"Can't we worry about it later?" she asked. "It *is* only a car."

"It's more than just a car!" Jim said, his voice rising. "It's a member of my family!"

Susan paused a moment to calm herself. Then she said, "Jim, everyone is here. What do you want me to do?"

"Just wait, *please*! I'll be there as soon as I can. Will you wait?"

"Sure," Susan sighed. "But only because I don't want to tell anyone that I've been stood up because of a car."

"Well, one thing is obvious," the policeman said to Jim. "You really are getting married."

Now only two cars stood between Herbie and destruction. The sound of a car being mashed into a cube made Herbie start to tremble. But then the forklift operator stopped working to light up a cigarette.

*　　　*　　　*

"Where could they have taken him?" Jim asked frantically.

"Almost anywhere," the policeman said, getting into his car. "We've already called in a stolen car report. We'll let you know if anything turns up."

The radio in the police car crackled. A tinny voice reported, "Report of gunshots was a false alarm. Repeat, gunshots at Rainey's Wrecking Yard was a false alarm. It was a car backfiring."

Jim stared out into space. It took a few seconds for the police report to register on his brain.

"Do you want a lift to the chapel?" the policeman asked.

"Backfiring?" Jim said, not hearing the question. "A car backfiring? At a wrecking yard?"

"Are you all right, sir?" the policeman asked.

Again Jim didn't answer. He opened the back door of the patrol car, got in, and closed the door behind him.

"Officer!" he said. "If you've ever played a long shot, play one now! Take me there, please!"

"Take you where?"

"To that wrecking yard! It could be a matter of life and death!" Jim screamed.

The roof light of the car began to spin, and the siren went on. Other drivers cleared the way for the patrol car.

As they left the business district, Herbie was next in line for the crusher.

Chapter 13 _____

Rainey signaled to the forklift operator, who turned his machine around in Herbie's direction. When he got into position, he slid the huge fingers of the forklift under Herbie's frame.

Herbie trembled uncontrollably as the steel fingers reached under his body and closed tightly around him.

The forklift raised Herbie off the ground. His trembling increased as he was swung around to the top of the compacting machine.

Rainey waved to the forklift operator. Herbie was lowered into the machine. Then the forklift released its grip.

Herbie was on the crushing platform. A

huge metal slab stood ready to be lowered onto his roof.

Water squirted on Herbie's windshield as the walls got closer. His windshield wipers slapped back and forth crazily.

Rainey gripped the lever that controlled the moving slab. He leaned forward to increase the pressure. Suddenly, another hand gripped his—and pulled the lever back.

Rainey looked up in surprise. "What do you think you're doing?" he roared at Jim.

Then he noticed the two policemen standing at Jim's sides. "Uh, can I help you gentlemen?" he asked.

"Get that car out of there!" Jim demanded.

Rainey looked at the policemen. Then he pulled back on the lever.

The four of them watched as Herbie was carefully lifted out of the compactor. When he was safely back on the ground, Jim quickly ran over to him.

"Easy, Herbie, old buddy," he said, patting the hood to calm the shaking car. "It's okay, Herbie. Nothing more to worry about. We're together again."

Jim looked up to see the two policemen talking with Rainey. He walked over to them.

"I'm telling ya," Rainey said. "I don't

know who he was. All I know is, he kept giving me money."

"That could be anybody," Jim said.

"WHONNNNK!" Herbie called.

"On the other hand," Jim said knowingly, "it could be good old Uncle Randy. Herbie, can you get me to the chapel on time?"

"He might," the officer said, "with a police escort."

"What a shame," the minister said. "And we had such a splendid rehearsal yesterday."

He was standing outside the chapel door with Susan, Bo, and the kids. Bigelow and Elizabeth stood off to the side.

"So the shakes finally caught up with him," Bo said. "It doesn't mean he won't be here!"

Bigelow stepped up to Susan's waiting car and opened the door. He nodded to Susan.

"I'd stay and wait for him," Matthew said solemnly.

"We *all* would," Julie added.

"We all *have*," Susan said angrily. "Now it's time to go."

She pointed to the car door. Matthew and Julie slowly moved toward it.

"Aren't we gonna marry Jim?" Robbie asked.

"No, Robbie," Bigelow said sweetly. "But you have to look on the bright side. You still have your Uncle Randy."

He nudged Robbie into the backseat. Then he held the front door open for Susan.

"What about the honeymoon reservations?" Elizabeth asked.

"Cancel them!" Susan snapped. "There must be a groom somewhere who doesn't have cold feet!"

She got into the car. Bo and Elizabeth walked sadly to the parking lot. The minister shook his head glumly as he watched Bigelow drive Susan's car away.

There was another wedding party waiting inside the chapel door. The minister turned to nod at them, and dropped his book and his papers on the sidewalk. As he bent down to pick them up, two cars pulled up side by side near the chapel. The police car was on the outside. Both policemen waved to Jim and pulled away.

Herbie stopped in front of the minister and Jim jumped out. He bent down to help him pick up his things.

"It was such a lovely rehearsal," the minister was saying to himself. "I was looking forward to a beautiful wedding."

"So am I," Jim said, and they both stood up.

"Oh!" the minister said, recognizing him. "They've left." He motioned toward the chapel door. "My next wedding is already here."

Herbie's passenger door popped open. Jim looked from the wedding party to the car. Then he pulled the minister to the curb, and put him in the car.

"I'll have him back in fifteen minutes," he called to the befuddled party in the chapel. Then Herbie started up, and they were off.

Bigelow drove happily away from the chapel, chattering away to his silent audience.

"I've never said a word against him," he said. "And heaven knows I never would. But when a man puts a *car* before his bride-to-be, well—"

It was the loud, constant beeping that made him stop talking. As he looked in his rearview mirror, all three kids turned around to see where the noise was coming from.

"It's Jim!" Matthew said.

"Herbie's here!" Robbie cried.

"Too late!" Bigelow said, as Susan continued to stare straight ahead. "Too late, Douglas!" he shouted into the rearview mirror.

"He's got the minister with him!" Julie said.

"I don't care if he has the Church of England with him!" Bigelow sputtered, jamming his foot on the gas pedal. "He's too late!"

They pulled away from Herbie, but only for a second. Herbie let out a burst of speed, and he was right back on their tail.

"Mom!" Julie pleaded. "At least we could stop and hear what he has to say!"

"Never!" Bigelow yelled, as Susan stared ahead.

"Hey!" Matthew said, pointing ahead. "There's Herbie!"

Robbie looked at the parked car a block in front of them. Then he turned and looked out the back window.

"Then how did he get behind us?" he asked.

Bigelow looked at the VW ahead of him, and then shot a glance at the rearview mirror. As he neared the parked imitation, Herbie pulled up on his right side. Herbie swerved toward Susan's car, forcing Bigelow to jam on his brake and skid toward the left.

Bigelow came to a stop directly in front of the imitation. The kids rolled out of the car, and Jim jumped out of Herbie.

128

"Two Herbies!" Robbie said, looking from one to the other.

"*One* Herbie," Jim said, "and one imposter."

Bigelow and Susan got out of her car, and Jim rushed up to her.

"Honey," he said breathlessly, "this is the crazy story I was trying to tell you on the phone!"

Then he stopped and looked at Bigelow. "Unless somebody else wants to tell you about it," he added.

"Are you accusing me of something, Douglas?" Bigelow said angrily.

"We'll have a little chat," Jim said, "after the honeymoon."

"Don't listen to him, Susan!" Bigelow screamed. "I did *not* steal this miserable little car, and I resent the accusation!"

His face was bright red now, and he tore his collar open and waved his arms.

"I resent being accused of anything! I was not drunk! It was that miserable car that was drunk!"

The kids stared at him, open-mouthed. Susan looked from him to Jim and began to figure out what was going on.

"I know, I know!" Bigelow went on, the pitch of his voice getting higher and higher. "He prefers little old ladies! Well, let me tell you something! When *I* was a little old lady, he didn't prefer *me!*"

He stopped to gasp for breath and suddenly realized that everyone was staring at him. He also realized what he'd just been saying. He slapped his hands over his mouth to keep himself from saying any more.

"Reverend," Jim said, "we're ready to be married now."

Susan and the kids got into her car. Jim and the minister got into Herbie. Then both cars turned around and headed for the chapel.

"Susan!" Bigelow screeched. "He left you once! He'll leave you again! You're making a big mistake! I won't let you do it!"

He pulled open the door of the parked VW. He started it up, pulled out, and made a sharp U-turn.

Bigelow went half a block before he had to stop. The stink bomb went off, and the car was lost in a cloud of smoke. Bigelow staggered out, coughing and wheezing. He waved his fist in the direction of the two departing cars.

They were in a small park a few blocks from the chapel. Jim and Susan stood before the minister. The kids stood around them.

"I think we're ready," Jim said to the minister.

"Unfortunately," he responded, "I dropped my book in all the confusion."

"That's all right, Reverend," Jim said. "I think we can do this one by heart."

He took Susan's hand, and they looked into each other's eyes.

"Susan," he said, "I love you very much. I want to spend the rest of my life with you. I'll try hard to make a worthwhile life for us, and for Julie, Matthew, and Robbie."

"I love you, Jim," Susan said. "I'm so glad you came into our lives. I hope we have a long and caring life with each other. We'll be together in all that we do—Julie, Matthew, Robbie, you, and I . . . and Herbie."

The minister sighed and smiled. "There's really nothing I could add to that," he said. "Except—do you have the ring?"

"Ring?" Jim asked, blinking. He looked around, and Herbie caught his eye. He was wriggling his antenna.

"Just a minute," Jim said.

He walked over to Herbie and steadied the antenna. Then he unscrewed the ring that held the antenna in place. He slipped the ring over the antenna and hurried back to the group.

"My best man had the ring," he said with a grin. Then he slid the ring onto Susan's finger.

"Jim and Susan," the minister said, "may the Lord look upon you and fill your lives with happiness. I now pronounce you husband and wife."

Jim and Susan turned to each other and kissed.

Julie, Matthew, and Robbie cheered.

And Herbie tooted "Here Comes the Bride."